For Ryan...

PIE

Sarah Weeks

SCHOLASTIC INC.

No part of this publication may be reproduced, stored in a retrieval system,
or transmitted in any form or by any means, electronic, mechanical,
photocopying, recording, or otherwise, without written permission
of the publisher. For information regarding permission, write to Scholastic Inc.,
Attention: Permissions Department, 557 Broadway, New York, NY 10012.

This book was originally published in hardcover by Scholastic Press in 2011.

ISBN 978-0-545-27012-0

12   15 16 17 18/0

Printed in the U.S.A. 40
This edition first printing, May 2013

The text was set in Alisal.
Book design by Kristina Iulo

To my faithful readers,
because a book is like a pie —
the only thing more satisfying than cooking up the story
is knowing that somebody might be out there
eating it up with a spoon.

— SW

APPLE PIE

6 large apples
½ lemon
¼ cup light brown sugar
1 TBS flour or cornstarch
1 tsp cinnamon
¼ tsp cloves
¼ tsp nutmeg
¼ tsp ginger
1 TBS sweet unsalted butter
1 egg white
Cinnamon sugar

Fresh-picked fruit is always best, of course, but if
you have to use store-bought apples, look for crisp
varieties, like McIntosh or Granny Smith. Peel, core,
and cut them up, but don't worry about making the
pieces all the same size — apple pies look best when
they're lumpy! Squeeze lemon over the whole lot and
sprinkle with sugar, flour, and spices. Toss with two
forks and pour into unbaked, pricked piecrust. Dot
with butter and cover with top crust. Crimp edges,
cut vents in center of crust, and brush with egg
white. Sprinkle with plenty of cinnamon sugar. Bake
at 350 for one hour or until lightly browned.

Reminder: Doc Fyfe's favorite. (Birthday: September 27)
He prefers a streusel topping: 1 stick sweet butter, ½ cup
brown sugar, juice of a lemon, ½ cup flour, a handful of
chopped walnuts. Work it together with your fingers until nice
and crumbly. Sprinkle over apples before baking.

Chapter One

"Thank you very much."

Alice was standing beside the bed when her aunt Polly reached a trembling hand out from underneath the leopard-print bedspread (Polly *loved* leopard print) and pulled the girl close to whisper in her ear.

"Thank you very much."

They would be the last words Polly Portman, the Pie Queen of Ipswitch, ever spoke.

• • •

Polly Portman was a natural born pie maker. When she was little, even her mud pies were a cut above what anyone else in the sandbox was doing. Recognizing her talent, Polly's mother, Hester Portman, bought her daughter a little wooden rolling pin, set her on a tall red kitchen stool, and taught her how to roll out her first piecrust.

As Polly grew, so did her pie-making skills. She learned that scalding milk before adding eggs would ensure a custard as smooth as silk and that whipped cream should be whisked just shy of the point where it would turn to butter. She became an expert at cutting narrow strips of pie dough and weaving them into lattice crusts and discovered that if she raised the oven rack a notch when baking a meringue, the peaks would turn the color of toasted marshmallow. When Polly grew tired of the recipes in her mother's cookbooks, she began to make up recipes of her own, learning to trust her instincts and *listen* to the ingredients. She could pinch a blueberry, sniff a peach, or take a bite of an apple and know exactly how much sugar to use and whether a grating of fresh nutmeg, a squirt of lemon juice, or a dash of salt would enhance the flavor of the fruit. Polly had a gift for baking pies, and she poured her heart and soul into every one she made.

Anyone who tasted one of her pies always said the same thing—"You ought to open up your own shop, Polly!" So when her parents passed away, leaving everything they had to Polly and her younger sister, Ruth, Polly set aside half of her inheritance to live on, and the other half she invested in a dilapidated old storefront on the corner of Windham and Main in downtown Ipswitch, Pennsylvania.

Almost as handy with a hammer as she was with a rolling pin, Polly converted the upstairs into a cozy little apartment. Downstairs she built the pie shop she had always dreamed of having. It wasn't much to look at, just a big room with a long wooden counter, a couple of tin pie safes, and a secondhand oven she'd picked up at an auction, but as far as Polly was concerned, the place was perfect. Being a humble person, she gave her pie shop a humble name — PIE.

When PIE first opened its doors in 1941, Alice Anderson hadn't even been born yet, but people in Ipswitch loved to tell the story, so she'd heard it a million times. The night before the opening, Polly was too excited to sleep. Finally she gave up, got dressed, and went downstairs to the shop. While everyone else in town was still snoring in bed, Polly tied on her favorite apron (leopard print, of course) and began to bake. By the time dawn spread its buttery light across the morning sky, there was a row of beautiful pies cooling on the counter and a crowd of people outside the door waiting to buy them.

Polly had put a great deal of thought into the pies she made that morning. She wanted to make sure there was some-thing for everyone. For the berry enthusiast, she made triple berry pies filled with a medley of ripe blackberries, raspber-ries, and blueberries. For the more adventurous she created green tomato and Concord grape pies. Of course there were traditional pies like cherry, apple, and rhubarb with golden top crusts spread like quilts over the sweet warm fillings, and cream pies galore — chocolate, coconut, and banana. Polly even managed to come up with something for the pie lover worried about an expanding waistline — a refreshingly tart low-calorie buttermilk pie, sprinkled with fresh nutmeg.

The citizens of Ipswitch had been sampling Polly Portman's pies at church picnics and 4-H fairs for years, so they were tickled pink that she had finally opened a shop of her own. Their delight, however, quickly turned to concern when they discovered Polly wasn't planning to sell the pies she made in her shop; she was planning to give them away.

"Why on earth would I charge people money for something that brings me so much pleasure?" Polly asked Reverend Flowers when he stopped by the shop one day to pay her a visit.

"How else do you expect to stay in business, my dear?" he responded, a touch of worry creasing his brow.

"You of all people should know the answer to that." Polly laughed, then handed the reverend a sour cherry pie, which she happened to know was his favorite, and sent him on his way.

At first, people couldn't decide what to do about Polly's pie shop. As much as they loved her pies, nobody was comfortable with the idea of getting one for free. So when no amount of coaxing could convince Polly to accept money for her pies, her friends and neighbors came up with an idea for another way to pay her. Every morning when Polly came downstairs to the shop, she would find an assortment of fresh ingredients waiting for her on the doorstep. One day there might be a basket of lemons and three dozen eggs, the next day a bushel of apples, a pot of fresh cream, and a giant sack of flour. Whatever people brought her, Polly would put to good use, and in no time at all, every surface in the shop would be covered with delicious fruit pies bursting at the seams with sweet juice, delicate silk pies sprinkled with curls of milk chocolate, chess pies with caramelized cornmeal tops, and custard pies piled so high with whipped cream it looked like they had snowdrifts sitting on top of them.

Word of Polly Portman's remarkable pie shop spread when a reporter from *The Ipsy News* wrote an article about it. The Associated Press picked up the story and pretty soon people from all over the country were flocking to the corner of Windham and Main to experience PIE for themselves. They came bearing raspberries from Oregon, sugarcane from Louisiana, pecans from Texas, and cherries from Michigan. Day after day, people flocked to the shop, and whatever they brought with them, Polly would turn into pies.

Alice came along in March of 1945. She was the apple of her aunt Polly's eye. The two of them spent a great deal of time together at the pie shop. When Alice was a toddler, Polly would sit her on the tall red stool—the very same stool Polly had sat on as a child—and give Alice a lump of pie dough to play with while she baked. Later on, when Alice was old enough to help, Polly would give her little jobs to do, like crumbling the brown sugar for streusel or pulling the stems off cherries.

Alice spent every Saturday at the pie shop. Polly taught her how to weave a lattice and how to crimp the edges of a crust by pinching the dough between her thumbs. Alice was happy to help, but she wasn't really interested in learning how to bake pies. She had inherited neither her aunt's talent nor her passion for it. The reason she came to the pie shop was to be near Polly, and there was nothing she loved more than sitting on the tall red stool, watching the magic happen.

Polly always began by making the crusts. She would mix up a big batch of dough before Alice even arrived, then while Alice cracked walnuts or hulled strawberries, Polly would carefully roll out the rounds of dough, folding each one over her forearm before gently transferring it into a tin pie plate. When she was finished, she would prick the bottom of the crusts five times with a fork, then drop a handful of dried beans into half of them — to keep the dough from cracking while they prebaked for cream pies — and set the rest of the crusts aside to be filled with fruit or custard and baked later.

Working side by side at the long wooden counter, time flew by and Alice and Polly never seemed to run out of things to talk about. The air was filled not only with the delicious smell of baking pies, but with the sweet sound of laughter. Pie after pie after pie went into the oven, and no sooner would Polly pull them out than the little silver bell over the door would jingle, merrily announcing the arrival of another hungry customer. Polly greeted each and every one with a sunny smile and a warm welcome. People loved coming to PIE, but to Alice it was much more than just a pie shop. It was a home away from home, a safe place where she could truly be herself.

"I'll miss you, Aunt Polly," Alice would say at the end of the day when it was time for her to go.

"I'll miss you even more," Polly would tell her. Then she'd hand Alice a pie to bring home to her parents, kiss her on the forehead, and send her on her way.

• • •

Ipswitch, Pennsylvania, is a small town. Always was. Always will be. In July of 1955, the population was one hundred and sixty-two. People who visited Ipswitch often commented on what a happy place it was. Folks whistled when they walked down the street, neighbors were downright neighborly, and everyone seemed to be in a good mood. Well, almost everyone.

"Mama always favored Polly," Alice heard her mother complaining to her father one evening about a week or so before her aunt Polly passed. Alice's father had snuck out on the porch, hoping to read his newspaper in peace, but her mother had followed him there. It was a warm night, and with the windows open, Alice couldn't help but overhear her parents' conversation.

"Now, Ruthie," Alice's father said, "let's not open up that can of worms again."

"Well, it's true, George. All of that fuss over Polly's talent. I had talent, too, you know."

"Of course you did, dear."

"But did Mama even notice? No, she was too busy falling all over Polly and those stupid pies of hers."

Alice's father licked his lips. He had eaten a big slice of one of Polly's pies that very day. Chocolate cream. His favorite. The creamy filling was made from Dutch cocoa powder, eggs, sugar, and fresh whole milk stirred over a low flame until it thickened into a sweet, glossy brown pudding. Once it was cool, Polly spooned it into a baked crust and slathered the top with whipped cream sprinkled with curls of milk chocolate.

"Those pies are what's keeping this roof over our heads," he pointed out.

"You call this a roof?" Alice's mother snorted. "We could be living in a mansion if it weren't for Polly's selfishness."

"Keep your voice down, dear," her father said. "You don't want Alice to hear."

"I don't care if she hears. She's got stars in her eyes just like everyone else in this town. I'm tired of people acting like Polly Portman is some kind of a saint. If you ask me, she's just plain selfish. Not to mention crazy. Who in their right mind turns down the chance to be a millionaire?"

Alice heard the snap and rustle of her father's newspaper as he shook it open. He'd been down this road before and knew there was no point in arguing.

"Ten minutes, Ruthie — that's all I'm asking for," he said. "Mickey Mantle hit three homers against the Senators last night. At least let me read the sports page."

"Go ahead and read your paper, George," said Alice's mother. "But mark my words and mark them good — when old high-and-mighty Polly Portman finally kicks the bucket, she had better set things right with this family."

Alice stopped listening at that point and plugged her ears. She knew what "kicking the bucket" meant and she didn't want to think about that happening. Aunt Polly was her rock, her favorite person in the world, the only one she felt she could really count on. Things between Alice and her mother had never been easy. No matter how hard Alice tried to please her, she always got the feeling that her mother was disappointed. And the only thing her father seemed to care about was being left alone to read his newspaper. Alice couldn't imagine what life would be like without her aunt Polly. Little did she know how soon she would have to find out.

• • •

Polly Portman single-handedly put Ipswitch on the map. Her untimely death came as a terrible shock, not only to Alice but to the whole town. People wept openly on the street, a mountain of flowers collected on the doorstep of the pie shop, and the good citizens of Ipswitch prepared to lay their beloved pie queen to rest. The night before the funeral, Alice cried herself to sleep, and as she tossed fitfully in her bed, a big green Chevrolet rolled down the dark streets of Ipswitch, pausing on the corner of Windham and Main for a moment to idle outside Polly Portman's famous pie shop. The leopard-print curtains in the window were drawn and the sign on the door said CLOSED.

"*Never again,*" the driver whispered.

Then the car pulled away from the curb and disappeared into the night.

COCONUT CREAM PIE

Filling:

2 cups coconut milk	⅔ cup shredded coconut
½ cup sugar	1½ tsp coconut extract
3 TBS cornstarch	½ tsp vanilla
pinch salt	1 baked pie shell
3 large egg yolks	

In medium saucepan, whisk together coconut milk, sugar, cornstarch, and salt. Bring to boil over medium heat, whisking constantly until you feel like your arm's going to fall off. Remove from heat and in a medium bowl lightly whisk egg yolks until frothy. Whisk ¼ of the warm milk mixture into the egg yolks and then return mixture to saucepan. Whisking constantly, heat mixture until it starts to thicken, about one minute more. Stir in shredded coconut, coconut extract, and vanilla. Pour into a bowl, cover surface with waxed paper, and chill.

Topping:

1¼ cup heavy cream	⅛ tsp coconut extract
⅔ cup shredded coconut	⅛ tsp vanilla
2 TBS sugar	

Toast coconut and set aside to cool. Pour prepared coconut custard into baked pie shell. Whip cream until it forms soft peaks, stir in sugar and extracts. Spread topping over pie and press toasted coconut on top.

Reminder: Do not leave unattended on windowsill to cool. Squirrels LOVE coconut!

Chapter Two

The whole town of Ipswitch came to Polly Portman's funeral. A photographer from *The Ipsy News* was there with his camera and there were reporters from several different newspapers milling around outside. The Honorable Mayor Needleman himself was sitting in the pew behind Alice and her parents, wearing a dark gray suit and a pair of very shiny black wing tip shoes. His wife, Melanie Needleman, sat beside him in an elegant hat made of feathers. Their eleven-year-old daughter, Nora, who was in Alice's grade at school, was there, too, wearing a miniature version of the same hat her mother had on. Alice didn't care much for Nora Needleman. Being the mayor's daughter, Nora sometimes gave the impression that she thought she was better than other kids.

Alice had been crying her eyes out for two solid days. Her nose was as red as Rudolph's and she felt like a slice of Swiss cheese inside, all limp and full of holes. Her mother was sitting next to her, wringing a handkerchief like she was trying to strangle it, and on her mother's other side sat Alice's father, looking utterly miserable in an itchy wool suit. Just as Reverend Flowers was gearing up to deliver the eulogy, a boy named Charlie Erdling showed up and squeezed into the seat beside Alice.

"Sorry about your auntie," he whispered.

Apparently he didn't know that only family members were supposed to sit in the front row at a funeral. Alice's mother gave Charlie a dirty look, but he didn't seem to notice. Alice didn't care if he sat there or not. She was too sad to care about anything anymore. Reverend Flowers cleared his throat and began to talk about all the good things Polly Portman had done for Ipswitch and how much everybody had loved her.

"Who among us has not benefitted from the bounty of Polly's gifts? Her ready smile, her generosity of spirit, and, of course, her delicious pies." His eyes grew moist and his voice trembled with emotion as he continued, "Thanksgiving at the parsonage will never be the same without one of her sublime pecan pies gracing the table."

All around her, people startled snuffling back tears and blowing their noses like foghorns, but Alice was all cried out, so when she felt the lump start to rise in her own throat, she looked around for something to distract her and settled on Charlie Erdling's dirty fingernails.

Alice had known Charlie for most of her life, but they weren't friends. Like Nora Needleman, he'd been in her class at school that year. Charlie was tall for his age and skinny. He had gigantic feet and bright orange hair that he wore in a flattop, the sides clipped so close to his head you could see the pinkness of his scalp showing through. Polly Portman had hired Charlie from time to time to do odd jobs, like emptying the trash or toting groceries home from the store. As Alice studied his fingernails, each with a little crescent of black grease wedged beneath it, she found herself wondering if anyone in the Erdling household had ever heard of soap and a fingernail brush.

When Reverend Flowers finally stepped down from the pulpit, Charlie poked Alice in the ribs with a pointy elbow and jerked his thumb toward the front of the church, where Polly's coffin sat with the lid propped open.

"You gonna pay your respects to your auntie now?" he asked.

Alice shuddered. The last thing she wanted to do was look at Aunt Polly's body lying stiff and cold in that long wooden box. She hoped her aunt's spirit was far away, happily baking pies for a bunch of hungry angels up in heaven.

"You go ahead, if you want," Alice said, slumping down in her seat. "I think I'll sit here for a while."

Alice's parents paid their respects first, followed by Mayor Needleman, whose wife managed to orchestrate things so that the mayor would be the one to take Alice's mother's arm and lead her up the aisle while the photographer from *The Ipsy News* snapped pictures for the paper. The mayor was running for reelection, and his wife, who also happened to be his campaign manager, knew a good photo opportunity when she saw one. Only the week before, the mayor had posed for a picture with Polly in the pie shop, for an article that was to appear in *LIFE* magazine. Alice had learned this not from her aunt Polly, who was modest about such things, but from the mayor's wife, whom Alice and her mother had run into at the grocery store in the frozen-food aisle one day.

"Did you hear about it, Ruth?" Mrs. Needleman had bragged. "*LIFE* magazine. With the election coming up in November . . . well, the timing couldn't be more perfect. Henry of course didn't even want to do the interview — he hates talking to reporters almost as much as he hates giving speeches — but I told him only a fool would turn down that kind of publicity. You know what they say: One minute the mayor's office, the next minute the Oval Office! *President Needleman* does have a nice ring to it, doesn't it?"

Alice's mother was not a big fan of Melanie Needleman, whom she found self-centered and too tightly wound. As Mayor Needleman led Alice's mother up the aisle of the church after the funeral, his wife followed a few steps behind him, brushing dandruff flakes off his shoulders in between the bursts of flashbulbs. Mrs. Needleman was so concerned with the task at hand that she didn't notice the elderly white-haired woman in a black veil attempting to get past her. Finally the woman, leaning heavily on her cane, tapped Mrs. Needleman on the shoulder with a gloved hand.

"Do you mind, dearie?" she croaked. "I'm in a bit of a hurry."

Melanie Needleman stepped to one side and let the woman pass, then she returned her attention to her husband's dandruff. A few minutes later, a big green Chevrolet pulled out of the church parking lot and drove off in the direction of the pie shop.

Alice didn't feel like going outside, where she'd have to listen to a bunch of people blubbering about how much they were going to miss her aunt Polly and her pies. Nobody was going to miss Polly as much as Alice would. There were still plenty of people left in the church paying their respects. Dressed in black, making their way single file down the aisle, they reminded Alice of a trail of ants. Looking down, she saw that her shoe had come undone and bent to tie it, making a double knot this time to be sure that it held. When she sat back up, she noticed a tall woman in a voluminous black dress looming over her aunt's open casket. The woman wore a large ring on the second finger of her right hand that sparkled and flashed in the sunlight filtering into the church through the high arched windows above. Even though Alice couldn't see her face, she knew who it was right away. Miss Gurke, the principal from her school, always dressed that way, in clothes so loose you could have fit a second person inside and still had room to spare.

Alice was afraid of Miss Gurke. In addition to the strange way she dressed, there was an oily glistening quality to her skin that reminded Alice of a snake. Miss Gurke's pet peeve was tardiness. She would stand inside the front door, grabbing kids by the hoods of their jackets and frog-marching them straight down to her office if they arrived so much as a second after the bell had rung. Since kindergarten, Alice had always made it a point to get to school at least fifteen minutes early.

As Alice watched from her seat in the pew, Miss Gurke bowed her head, resting both hands on the edge of the casket. When she had finished paying her respects, she did something curious. Instead of turning away, she leaned over the casket and slipped her hand into it, almost as if she intended to lift Polly's head up and kiss her good-bye. She must have reconsidered, Alice decided, because Miss Gurke quickly jerked her hand back out and walked away, hurrying up the aisle and out of the church without looking back.

Alice stayed until the whole place had emptied out and the last of the mourners had left. It was peaceful then, and quiet, a perfect time to reflect on the many special moments she and her aunt Polly had shared together.

She recalled a time she'd stopped by the pie shop on her way home from school one day and found her aunt squeezing lemons for a batch of lemon chess pies.

"Can I go fishing?" asked Alice, happily hopping up on the red stool.

Polly finished squeezing the last of the lemons and passed the bowl to Alice. Then she handed her a fork.

"Fish away," she told her.

"Mom says you could be a millionaire if you wanted to be," Alice said as she began to fish out the slippery white lemon seeds with the fork and drop them into the little dish her aunt had placed on the counter beside her. "Don't you want to be rich?"

"I'm already rich in all the ways that count," said Polly. "And so is your mother, even if she doesn't know it yet."

"If you say so," said Alice, "but I hope you've got that recipe locked up someplace safe."

"Don't worry." Polly smiled and tapped the side of her head. "I've got it right here."

While she waited for Alice to finish, Polly absentmindedly fiddled with the brass key that hung on a chain around her neck. She was forever doing that, tucking the key into the top of her blouse or tugging on it while she was talking. Alice loved the way it would sometimes dangle down and twirl, catching in the light as her aunt slipped a pie into the glowing oven. It was the only key to the pie shop door and Polly always wore it around her neck for safekeeping.

When the last of the seeds had been removed from the lemon juice, Polly sent Alice to the pantry to get some sugar, while she went and fetched the basket of fresh brown eggs someone had left on the doorstep that morning.

"If I ask you something, do you promise you'll give me an honest answer, Aunt Polly?" Alice asked, resting her elbows on the counter while she watched her aunt carefully rinse off the eggs.

"Of course," Polly told her. "Ask me anything."

"Do I have an active imagination?"

"Absolutely," Polly said, cracking an egg smartly against the rim of a bowl.

"That's what I was afraid of," said Alice with a sigh.

"What do you mean?" Polly asked. "An active imagination is a wonderful thing to have."

"Mom doesn't think so," Alice confided. "She thinks it's annoying."

"Pish posh," Polly said, tossing aside the empty shell and grabbing another egg.

"Sometimes I make up little songs," said Alice. "Mom says that's especially annoying."

Polly got a faraway look in her eyes. "Your mother used to sing all the time when she was a little girl. She had the voice of an angel."

"Really?" Alice couldn't remember ever having heard her mother sing.

"It was a joy to listen to her," said Polly.

"Mom says I'm tone-deaf," Alice said.

"Join the crowd." Polly laughed sympathetically. "I couldn't tell the difference between flat and sharp if my life depended upon it. So how about singing me one of your little songs?"

"Right now?" Alice asked.

Polly nodded, so Alice jumped off the red stool, cleared her throat, and sang a song she made up right on the spot.

Aunt Polly's pies are hot and round,
Eat 'em in a chair or sittin' on the ground,
Huckleberry, blackberry, peach, and prune,
Eat 'em with a fork or eat 'em with a spoon.

When Alice had finished singing, Polly threw her arms around her.

"Bravo!" she cried.

"I've never heard of a prune pie," Alice told her. "But sometimes you have to stick strange things into songs to get the rhymes to work."

"I loved it," Polly said. "Prunes and all. And I love you, too, Alice."

"I wish I could sing better," Alice said.

"It's important to be grateful for the gifts we have," Polly told her. "You are a wonderful songwriter. Don't you ever forget that."

Alice felt all warm and gooey inside, like one of her aunt Polly's pies. She wanted to stay there in the pie shop forever. Aunt Polly was the only other person Alice knew who liked cream cheese and olive sandwiches. That's what they had for lunch the day Polly died. It was a Friday in the middle of July, school was out, and Alice had come over to the shop to help her aunt string a bushel of rhubarb for rhubarb pie. At noon they took a break and ate their sandwiches upstairs, sitting across from each other at the kitchen table. Then Polly said she wasn't feeling well and wanted to lie down for a bit. Alice covered her with the leopard-print quilt that lay folded on the foot of the bed, and as she bent to kiss her aunt's smooth cheek, Polly Portman whispered those final words, *"Thank you very much."* By morning she was gone.

• • •

Alice wasn't sure how long she'd been sitting there alone in the church thinking about her aunt Polly, but when she stood up, she found that her left foot had gone to sleep, so she jiggled it a little to wake it up. She had every intention of going outside to find her parents, but for some strange reason, her feet carried her down the aisle and deposited her right in front of her aunt's open casket instead. She had to admit, they'd done a good job of fixing her up. Her hair was curled and she had on a nice shade of pink lipstick. But as Alice stood there gazing down at her aunt Polly, she got the strangest feeling inside. She couldn't quite put her finger on it, but something was not right.

BUTTERMILK PIE

1 9-inch pie tin, lined with unbaked piecrust
3 large eggs
¾ cup sugar
3 TBS flour
1½ cups low-fat buttermilk
1 tsp vanilla
3 TBS fresh lemon juice
1 tsp grated lemon rind
1 tsp butter, melted
½ tsp ground nutmeg

Preheat oven to 350. Cover unbaked pie shell with parchment paper or a coffee filter. Press down to fit and toss in a handful of dried beans. Place weighted shell in preheated oven and bake for 10 minutes. Remove from oven and empty out beans. Discard parchment and set pastry shell aside.

Raise oven to 375. Beat eggs and sugar until light and lemony colored. Add flour and beat until well mixed. Add buttermilk, vanilla, lemon juice, lemon rind, and butter. Pour into baked crust and dust with nutmeg. Bake in preheated 375-degree oven for 25-30 minutes. Cool slightly on wire rack before serving.

Reminder: Doris Kaperfew's favorite. (Birthday: August 12)

Chapter Three

There were a couple of surprising things about Polly Portman's will. The first was that she left the pie shop and all of its contents to Reverend Flowers, with instructions that he was to use it in whatever way he chose to help raise funds for the church. Alice's mother was fit to be tied.

"She's thumbing her nose at us even from the grave," she shouted angrily. "We're *family*. By all rights the pie shop should be ours."

Her dark mood quickly lifted, however, when Polly's lawyer, Mr. Ogden, called the house.

"He's asked to speak to you, Alice," Alice's father said, handing her the phone.

Mrs. Anderson could barely contain herself, breathing down Alice's neck and whispering instructions into her free ear as she strained to hear what Mr. Ogden was saying on the other end of the line. By the time Alice hung up, her mother was practically beside herself.

"What did he say?" she cried. "Is it good news? Tell us everything."

"He wants me to come down to his office," Alice said.

"*And?*" her mother urged, eyes gleaming.

"He said Aunt Polly left me something in her will and that I should come as soon as possible to get it."

"Did you hear that, George?" Alice's mother said excitedly. "I'll just run upstairs and put on some lipstick."

"He wants me to come alone, Mom," Alice said.

"Oh," said Alice's mother.

"Did he say anything else?" her father asked, and Alice could tell by the little pink spots on his cheeks that he was starting to get excited now, too.

"Well, it was kind of hard to hear, 'cause Mom was talking to me at the same time, but I know it has something to do with Aunt Polly's piecrust recipe."

"Great merciful heavens!" Alice's mother exclaimed, clapping both hands to her cheeks. "Do you realize what this means? Polly has finally set things right. She's left you the recipe! We'll sell it to the highest bidder and kiss all our cares good-bye." Tears of joy filled her eyes as she threw back her head and shouted, *"We're going to be rich!"*

Alice's father just kept shaking his head and saying, "Well, I'll be a monkey's uncle."

For many years, Alice's father had worked for the Hoover Company, peddling vacuum cleaners door-to-door. It was not the job of his dreams, so when PIE began to attract tourists to Ipswitch, he heard the sound of opportunity knocking. With Polly's blessing, he set up a souvenir stand next to the shop, where he sold key chains shaped like rolling pins, leopard-print pot holders, and aprons with a picture of Polly's smiling face embroidered on the front and the slogan, *"Hey, Polly, what's your secret?"* stitched beneath it.

It was the question everybody asked, and the answer nobody knew: the secret to Polly Portman's perfect piecrust.

"It's by far the flakiest!"

"Ever so crisp!"

"Light as a feather!"

Anyone who doubted this high praise had only to look under Polly's bed. That's where she kept her Blueberry medals.

"Aunt Polly, how come you keep your medals under the bed?" Alice had asked one day.

"I keep them under the bed so I won't have to look at them," Polly said.

"Why don't you want to look at them?"

"I'm afraid I might get a swelled head," she said with a wink. "And then I wouldn't be able to wear my favorite hat anymore."

Polly's favorite hat was a leopard-print cloche she'd purchased from the Sears catalogue the year she won her first

Blueberry Award. The Blueberry Award was established in 1922 to celebrate the most distinguished contribution to American pie making. Each year during the month of August, people from all over the country would box up their pies and deliver them to the Blueberry committee for consideration. The committee members would carefully evaluate the pies, "Blueberry Buzz" would spread as the top contenders emerged, "Mock Blueberry" clubs would choose their own favorites, and finally on the first Monday in September, amid a great deal of fanfare, the Blueberry committee would announce the winner. Polly had never considered entering the contest. She baked because it made her happy, and as far as she was concerned, that was reward enough.

Then, early one August morning, a woman from St. Petersburg, Florida, by the name of Harriet Melcher arrived in Ipswitch carrying a five-pound coconut in her purse. Later that same day, she boarded the train back to St. Petersburg holding a cardboard box containing half a coconut cream pie. She'd eaten the other half earlier in the day and her hands were still shaking with excitement.

Polly would never have entered one of her pies in the contest herself, but Harriet Melcher happened to be on the Blueberry committee that year and, after tasting Polly's coconut cream pie, she took the liberty of bringing it—or what was left of it—to the committee herself. This is how it came to pass that at six o'clock in the morning on Monday,

September 7, 1942, Polly Portman received a phone call. The excited voice on the other end of the line belonged to Harriet Melcher.

"Good morning, Miss Portman! On behalf of the committee, I am pleased to inform you that you've just been awarded the 1942 Blueberry medal for your outstanding coconut cream pie. We look forward to seeing you at the award ceremony."

Polly was delighted that the committee had enjoyed her pie, but the idea of winning a prize for it made her feel very uncomfortable, so much so that she tried to turn it down.

"The Blueberry is the most coveted award in the field of pie baking, Miss Portman. You have no idea how many people would *kill* to be in your shoes," Harriet Melcher told her.

"What an awful thought!" Polly exclaimed.

"The ceremony is in Philadelphia this year — just a hop, skip, and a jump away from you. Everyone will be so disappointed if you don't come."

Not wanting to seem ungrateful, Polly finally agreed to accept the award and to attend the ceremony in Philadelphia. She even ordered herself a new hat from Sears. A few weeks later, she wore the leopard-print cloche to the American Pie Makers Association conference, where she delivered a heartfelt four-word acceptance speech — *"Thank you very much."*

Things changed after Polly Portman won the Blueberry Award. All kinds of people started showing up at the shop with ideas about how she could expand PIE or turn it into a national chain. One eager businessman came all the way from Hong Kong to unveil his plans to build a giant factory where Polly's pies would be mass-produced, frozen, and shipped all over the world. He told Polly she would be so rich, she'd never have to bake again.

"Why on earth would I want that?" she laughed. Then she handed him the green tomato pie she'd noticed him eyeing earlier and showed him to the door.

Just as the hoopla surrounding Polly's Blueberry Award began to die down, she won another one — this time for her buttermilk pie. Once again, she hadn't entered the contest herself, but the word was out about Polly's pie-making skills, and after that there was no stopping her. Each September like clockwork the call would come and Polly would put on her leopard-print hat and go off to wherever the APA conference was being held that year to deliver the same heartfelt four-word speech — *"Thank you very much."*

Polly Portman won thirteen Blueberry medals in a row — something no pie maker before or since has ever done. Although she may not have wanted to cash in on her fame, Polly was more than happy to share her good fortune with her neighbors. With so many out-of-towners coming to Ipswitch to visit the pie shop, other local establishments began to experience a boon in their own businesses as well. The Ipsy Inn, which had been boarded up for years, was suddenly overflowing with guests. The coffee shop, the diner, and the drugstore raked in profits on everything from BLTs to aspirin tablets, and the city council voted to replace the old ENTERING IPSWITCH sign at the city limit with a fancy new one that said WELCOME TO IPSWITCH — THE PROUD HOME OF PIE. In the upper right-hand corner of the sign was a red circle with a number painted in the middle, which changed every time Polly Portman won another Blueberry Award. In 1955 the sign proudly proclaimed *13 Blueberries and Counting!*

Busloads of people arrived in Ipswitch every day to visit the pie shop, and time and again, Polly was asked to reveal the secret of her perfect piecrust.

"At least give us a hint," they would beg.

Even though Polly Portman was the kind of person who would have given you the shirt off her own back, she wouldn't tell anyone the recipe for her piecrust. Modesty would have prevented her from saying it, but she knew that the success of the town rested on her shoulders. Keeping the recipe a secret was part of what drew the tourists to Ipswitch, and without their patronage, many of the small businesses would have trouble staying afloat. Although Polly had no intention of sharing her secret any time soon, after the conversation with Alice about keeping the recipe safe, she had made arrangements for what would happen to the piecrust recipe when her time on earth came to an end.

Unfortunately, that time came much sooner than anyone expected, and as a result, things were about to change in Ipswitch . . . especially for Alice Anderson.

• • •

Mr. Ogden's office was only three blocks away from the Andersons' house, so Alice decided to ride her bike.

As she pedaled off down the street, she felt a song coming on.

I'd rather you were here of course,
I miss you through and through.
But thank you for the recipe,
Aunt Polly, I love you.

Singing about the recipe made Alice's stomach grumble. She had been so busy missing Aunt Polly, she hadn't realized she'd been missing something else, too — her pies. July was berry season. How good a slice of triple berry pie would taste right now, she thought. Aunt Polly used only the ripest berries, sweetening them with clover honey and a splash of vanilla. The thought of that pie, with its crispy golden crust and a scoop of homemade ice cream to go with it, made Alice feel so giddy, she missed the turn onto Maple Street and had to circle around and go back.

Mr. Ogden was sitting at his desk when Alice arrived. He was wearing a blue and white seersucker suit, a crisp white shirt, and a red tie. His pants were held up with a pair of suspenders the same shade of red as his tie, and, Alice noticed, he wore a pair of black wing tip shoes very much like the ones both Mayor Needleman and Reverend Flowers had worn to her aunt Polly's funeral. Alice knew they were called wing tips because her father also owned a pair, though he hadn't worn his to the funeral because he said they pinched his bunions. On the desk in front of Mr. Ogden lay a large white envelope, and on the other side of the desk sat two chairs, one of which was occupied by a brown leather case about the size of a bread box, decorated with leopard-print trim. Alice knew right away what was inside.

"Hello, Lardo," she whispered through the little mesh window sewn into one end of the case.

Lardo was Polly Portman's grumpy old cat, and Alice was scared to death of him. Talk about nasty—Lardo would scratch and bite and hiss at anybody who came near him, except for Polly. He'd showed up filthy and half starved at the pie shop one day, and when no one came to claim him, Polly took pity on him and decided to let him stay. Thanks to a steady diet of fried sardines and sweet cream, he quickly tripled in size. His big fat belly hung so low it brushed the floor as he walked, but that wasn't the reason Polly decided to call him Lardo. She had assumed at first that he was a tabby cat, but after risking life and limb to bathe him and brush out his matted gray coat, she discovered that underneath all that dirt and soot, he was actually white. So Polly decided to name him after the whitest thing she could think of — vegetable shortening.

There was a big pantry in the back of the pie shop where Polly kept a supply of essential ingredients for her baking. Anyone who's ever made a pie knows that you can't make a crust without using some form of fat. Some people like butter, others prefer oil, but Polly Portman was a firm believer in vegetable shortening. She went through gobs of the glistening snow-white goop every week at the shop, and the brand she always used was called LARDO!

Most people wouldn't have tolerated, let alone loved, a cat with a rotten disposition like Lardo's, but Polly adored and doted on him. Each morning before she went downstairs to the shop, she would fry up three sardines and put them on a little blue china plate for Lardo. He wouldn't give her the satisfaction of seeing him eat the fish of course, but one of Polly's favorite things in the world was to come upstairs at the end of a long day of baking to find the little blue plate licked clean.

"You must be hungry," Alice said, peering into the carrying case at Lardo.

He narrowed his yellow eyes at her and hissed.

"Charming cat," sniffed Mr. Ogden.

Alice felt a guilty pang. Everyone had been so wrapped up in Polly's passing and in planning the funeral, they'd all completely forgotten about Lardo. He'd been cooped up in the empty pie shop for three days with nothing to eat. No wonder he was grumpy.

"Poor kitty," said Alice.

Another hiss, even louder than the last, emanated from the case.

"Getting him here was no easy feat," Mr. Ogden said. "It took me over an hour to pull him out from under the bed. As you can see, I did not escape unscathed."

He held up his hands, displaying an impressive array of Band-Aids.

"Don't take it personally," Alice told him. "Lardo doesn't like anybody."

Mr. Ogden looked at his watch and frowned.

"Have a seat, young lady," he told Alice, indicating the unoccupied chair across from him.

Alice did as he instructed, sitting on the very edge of the chair, in case Lardo tried to take a swipe at her through his carrying case.

"As I mentioned on the phone," Mr. Ogden began, "this matter concerns a certain *bequest*, a gift, which your aunt has made on your behalf."

"I know," Alice said, feeling a tiny flutter of excitement under her ribs as she imagined the celebration the Anderson family would be having at their house that evening.

Mr. Ogden paused, pressing his fingertips together.

"Before we proceed, I'd like to explain a few things about your aunt's will," he said. "I knew Polly for over fifty years. She was both a client and a friend. I will miss her, not to mention that remarkable Concord grape pie she used to make."

Mr. Ogden licked his lips, savoring the memory of the pie for a moment before continuing.

"When Polly asked me to supervise the execution of her will, which is to say, sign it in my office with the necessary witnesses, I was more than happy to do so. However, I feel that it's important that you know that the actual will itself was not prepared by me; it was written at home by your aunt in her own hand. After signing it before two witnesses — my secretary, Miss Lebson, and a gentleman by the name of Hammerschlacht — she sealed it in an envelope, which she instructed me to open only in the event of her death. I read it myself for the first time this morning."

"What did it say?" Alice asked, hoping that Mr. Ogden's answer would be a lot shorter than the long-winded speech he'd just delivered.

"We'll get to that in a minute," he said. "First I'd like to remind you that as your aunt's attorney, my role in this matter is merely to inform you of her intentions, not to explain the reasons for them, and to see that they are carried out in the manner in which she has requested. Do you understand?"

"I think so," Alice said, afraid that if she admitted she hadn't understood something, he'd feel the need to repeat the whole thing all over again.

"Very well," Mr. Ogden said. Then he cleared his throat and began to read the will out loud.

The document consisted of a single page, handwritten in blue ink. It took Mr. Ogden less than a minute to read it, and when he had finished, two things were perfectly clear:

Polly Portman had left her secret piecrust recipe to her beloved cat, Lardo.

And she had left her beloved cat, Lardo, to Alice.

GREEN TOMATO PIE

8 medium-size green tomatoes (watch out for worms!)
1 tsp grated lemon peel
Juice of 1 lemon
½ tsp salt
½ tsp ground cinnamon
¼ tsp nutmeg
¾ cup granulated sugar
2 TBS cornstarch
1 TBS unsalted butter

Peel and slice tomatoes. In a saucepan, combine
tomatoes with lemon peel, lemon juice, salt,
cinnamon, and nutmeg. Cook tomato mixture over
low heat, stirring constantly. Combine sugar and
cornstarch and add to tomato mixture. Cook until
clear, stirring constantly. Remove from heat. Add
butter and let stand until almost cooled. Pour into
unbaked pie shell, cover with top crust. Bake at 400
for 45 minutes, or until nicely browned.

*Note: Not everybody likes the idea of a tomato pie — call it a
"mock apple," and they'll gobble it down!*

Chapter Four

"Her cat?" Alice's mother shrieked after Alice returned home from Mr. Ogden's office with Lardo's carrying case balanced precariously on her handlebars. "Is this some kind of a joke? What about the recipe?"

How Alice dreaded being the one to have to deliver the news.

"She left it to Lardo, Mom."

"What do you mean, she left it to Lardo? How do you leave a recipe to a *cat*?"

"I don't know," Alice answered honestly. "Aunt Polly told me she kept the recipe in her head."

"Surely, Mr. Ogden explained it to you."

Alice told her mother what Mr. Ogden had said about how his job was only to inform her of what Polly had decided to do with the recipe, not to explain why.

"That's ridiculous," huffed Alice's mother. "I'm going to

call Mr. Ogden right now and get to the bottom of this nonsense."

Meanwhile, Alice's father was dealing with a completely different issue.

"*A-choo!*" he sneezed, the minute he laid eyes on Lardo. Highly allergic, even the word "cat" could set him off. "*A-choo! A-choo! A-CHOO!*"

Mrs. Anderson reappeared a few minutes later looking ashen. The phone call with Mr. Ogden had not gone well. Although he had confirmed that the piecrust recipe had indeed been passed on to Lardo, Polly Portman had provided absolutely no instructions in her will as to how this was to be accomplished.

"I should have known it was too good to be true," Alice's mother said, putting her head in her hands. "That recipe is worth millions, but Polly decided she'd rather throw it away than give it to us. Not only that, but without the pie shop, what good will the souvenir stand be now?"

"There, there, Ruthie, don't cry," said Mr. Anderson, comforting his wife. "I'm sure there's an explanation. Perhaps Mr. Ogden misplaced a page of the will."

Alice shook her head.

"There was only one page," she told her father.

"Still, there must be some reason she's done what she's done," he insisted, then he pinched his nose to stifle an oncoming sneeze.

"She hated me, George," Alice's mother wailed. "That's the reason."

"Aunt Polly didn't hate you, Mom," Alice said. "She didn't hate anyone."

"How can you defend her after what she's done?" her mother shouted through her tears. "Clearly your precious aunt didn't care about any of us. Not even you, Alice."

Her mother's words stung, even though, in her heart, Alice knew they couldn't be true. Aunt Polly had loved her. She was certain of that. Still, she couldn't help wondering what her aunt could have been thinking, leaving something so valuable to a cat.

"What are we going to do, George?" Alice's mother cried. "What are we going to *do*?"

"Take the cat up to your room, Alice," her father said quietly. "And find him something to do his business in. Your mother and I need to talk."

Aunt Polly had kept a covered cat box for Lardo in her bathroom on the floor under the sink. It was filled with sand and had a little hinged door in it so he could have privacy while he was inside. The best Alice could come up with was a cardboard shoe box, which she filled with ripped-up newspaper and placed in the corner of the room. She went downstairs to the kitchen and came back up with two little bowls, one for water, the other for tuna fish, which was the closest thing to sardines that she could find. Lardo was still

41

in the carrying case, watching her every move with his scary yellow eyes. Alice was afraid to get too close, so when she finally got up the nerve to let him out, she used a bent coat hanger to pull the zipper. The second the flap fell open, Lardo streaked out of the case and scooted under the bed, hissing all the way.

He stayed there for the rest of the day.

When six o'clock rolled around, Alice's stomach was rumbling like an empty garbage can rolling down a hill, but downstairs there was no sign of dinner. Her father was parked at the kitchen table, reading the newspaper. News travels fast in a small town like Ipswitch, and the headline read PIE QUEEN LEAVES SECRET RECIPE TO CAT.

"Where's Mom?" she asked.

"Gone to bed with a sick headache," he answered, reaching for a napkin to wipe his mouth. In front of him on the table was a half-eaten piece of pie.

"Where did that come from?" Alice asked.

"I found it in the back of the fridge," he said. "There's one piece left if you want it."

Alice crossed the room to the refrigerator and pulled open the door. On the bottom shelf between a jar of dill pickles and a head of iceberg lettuce sat a tin pie plate containing a single slice of lemon chiffon pie. It seemed like only yesterday that Alice had pricked the bottom of that pie shell five times with a fork, and sat on the tall red stool while Aunt Polly crushed gingersnaps and peeled thin yellow curls of lemon skin to decorate the top with.

"It's a little past its prime," commented Alice's father from behind his newspaper, "but still delicious."

Alice got a fork from the drawer and carried the pie tin upstairs, where Lardo was still hiding under the bed, the bowl of tuna fish untouched. Aunt Polly and Alice had been alike in many ways, but when it came to eating pie, they were opposites. Like most people, Aunt Polly would start at the front of the slice and work her way to the back, but Alice always began by breaking off the crisp edges of crust, then moving forward, saving the tip — her favorite part — for last.

Sitting cross-legged on the bed, Alice began to eat the pie. Having spent nearly a week in the fridge, the crust was not as crisp as it had once been, but when the first bite of lemony mousse hit her tongue, Alice closed her eyes and smiled.

"Why is it called *chiffon?*" she remembered having asked her aunt.

"Chiffon is a kind of fabric," Polly had explained. "Cool and silky and lighter than air."

"Like those little white puffs your breath makes when it's cold outside."

"Yes, sweet girl," said Aunt Polly, leaning over to kiss the top of Alice's head. "Exactly like that."

Each bite brought back more happy memories, until all too soon Alice had reached the end of the pie. The tip had always been her favorite part, but this time when she pierced the pale yellow triangle and brought it to her lips, a single tear rolled down her cheek. It would be the last time she would ever taste one of Aunt Polly's pies.

Later she put on her pajamas and brushed her teeth, then crawled under the covers and read for a while until her eyelids began to droop. It was eight thirty when she turned out the light, and after a minute she heard Lardo come out from under the bed and walk across the room. There was a full moon that night, so enough light was coming in through the window that Alice could see him gulping down the tuna in great, greedy bites. He must have been starving after three days alone in the apartment—probably scared, too. For the first time, it occurred to Alice that she and Lardo might have something in common.

"You miss her, too, don't you?" Alice whispered.

She had always been afraid of Lardo, but maybe with time she could learn to love him. After all, Aunt Polly had loved him. As she watched Lardo lick the last of the tuna fish from his whiskers, Alice felt another song coming on.

Three sardines on a little blue plate
All in a neat little line.
Now that Aunt Polly has left us,
Did you know that you're legally mine?

She sang it softly a couple of times, and tried to come up with a less technical sounding word than "legally," but it had been kind of a long day, and she ended up falling asleep.

· · ·

In the middle of the night, Alice was awakened by a noise. She turned on the light, wondering if maybe Lardo had knocked something over, prowling around in the dark. He was nowhere in sight and nothing in the room seemed out of place, so Alice decided she must have been dreaming. Feeling a little chill, she shivered, then dove under the covers and went back to sleep.

Alice was not the only one awake in the middle of the night that night. Mayor Needleman was suffering a bout of indigestion and had gotten up to make himself a Bromo-Seltzer. As he stood at the kitchen sink in his bathrobe, sipping the bubbling concoction, he happened to look out the window and see a big green Chevrolet roll by with the headlights turned off.

"Who on earth could that be at this hour?" he wondered, and then he burped loudly and went back to bed.

The next morning when Alice woke up, she discovered that Lardo had left an unpleasant little surprise *next* to the shoe box. She cleaned up the mess and, after carefully checking to make sure that the door was latched tight, went downstairs to get some breakfast for herself and to see if she could rustle up another can of tuna fish for Lardo.

"Achoo!" her father greeted her from behind his morning newspaper.

"Bless you," Alice said.

Alice's mother was standing near the sink, hunched over a big bowl, stirring something vigorously with a wooden spoon. As she stirred, white clouds of flour rose from the bowl and fell like a dusting of powdery snow on the floor at her feet. There was a carton of cream and a tin of cocoa powder sitting on the counter nearby.

Alice was pleased to see that her mother had recovered from her headache and was feeling up to doing a little cooking. She took this as a good sign.

"What are you making, Mom?" she asked.

Her father, his nose buried deep in the morning paper, shifted uncomfortably in his chair.

"Your mother's making a pie," he said.

"*A pie!?*" Alice exclaimed, unable to hide her shock.

Alice's mother turned, her scowling face smudged with flour. There were dark circles under her eyes. Clearly she hadn't slept.

"That's right," she said. "A pie. For the first time in thirteen years, somebody other than Polly is going to win the Blueberry, and I don't see any reason why it shouldn't be me."

Alice could think of a very good reason. As far as she knew, her mother had never made a pie in her life.

"Thanks to your aunt's *generosity*," her mother continued, "your father's out of a job, Reverend Flowers has the pie shop, and what do we have?"

"*A-choo!*" Alice's father sneezed right on cue.

"Precisely," said Mrs. Anderson bitterly. "So yes, I'm making a pie. And unlike my sister, when I win *my* Blueberry, I'll have the good sense to sell my recipe, not leave it to a cat."

She turned back to her bowl and resumed stirring.

"You don't need to do this, Ruthie," Alice's father said. "I'll put a call in to Hoover tomorrow. If they can't take me back, I'm sure I can find something else."

"You're not the only one who's going to be looking for work, George. Without PIE, everybody in town is going to be scrambling," said Alice's mother.

It was true. A lot of folks in Ipswitch were already worried. Dick Kaperfew, the owner of the Ipsy Inn, had gotten so many calls from people canceling reservations, he had only one guest room occupied at the moment. Business downtown had slowed to a snail's pace, the diner was so quiet you could hear a fork drop, and Melanie Needleman couldn't stop complaining about the impact Polly's death was going to have on her husband's campaign.

"If only she could have hung on until after the election," she'd said to the mayor just that morning over coffee. He'd nodded, pretending to listen, but his mind was elsewhere.

"Pumpkin," he'd said with a sigh.

His wife smiled, thinking it was a new term of endearment, but when she'd questioned him about it, the mayor had confessed that it was actually Polly Portman's pumpkin pie he'd been mooning over.

"I've had such an awful craving for it since she passed, it's driving me to distraction."

Mayor Needleman was not the only one in town who'd been suffering from pie withdrawal. Delores Evans, a cashier at the A&P, had been rushed to the emergency room that day with heart palpitations. The doctor sent her home with instructions to take two aspirin and to try not to think about banana cream pie.

"You remember the way Polly always made it," the mayor had gone on, "with that wonderful crumbly stuff on top."

"It's called streusel, Henry. It's extremely fattening."

"And delicious," he'd added wistfully.

Melanie Needleman had frowned at her husband.

"How can you think about pie at a time like this? The future of Ipswitch is hanging in the balance." But to be honest, she had been thinking about Polly's low-calorie buttermilk pie for days, wondering how on earth she would ever stick to her diet without it. It had even occurred to her that she might try making one for herself, which quickly led to a fantasy of what would happen if she entered her pie in a certain contest and won. A Blueberry in the family would do wonders to perk up the mayor's campaign!

Back at Alice's house, Alice's mother was having similar thoughts. She scooped some flour out of the canister and sprinkled it on the counter. Then she scraped the contents of the mixing bowl out onto the floured spot with a rubber spatula.

"Who knows?" she said. "After I win my Blueberry, maybe I'll open a shop of my own. Ha! That would show Polly. I mean, really, how hard can it be to make a pie?"

Alice had watched her aunt Polly make many pies, so she knew what pie dough was supposed to look like. It was not gray and wet like the gloppy mess her mother had just plopped down on the counter, but Alice knew better than to say anything.

"Has anyone seen the rolling pin?" asked Alice's mother, rummaging around in a drawer. "I know there's one in here somewhere."

There was a bag of raisin bread sitting on the table. Alice was hungry, so she took out a slice and popped it into the toaster.

"Do we have any more tuna fish?" she asked while she waited for the bread to toast. "Lardo ate a whole can of it last night. I think he likes it almost as much as fried sardines."

"Look in the cupboard," Alice's mother told her. "Behind the baked beans. But consider it his last meal."

"What do you mean?" Alice asked.

"I called the pound this morning and they're expecting us to drop him off at ten."

"Mom," said Alice, choosing her words carefully, since it was obvious her mother was in no mood to be crossed, "Aunt Polly gave Lardo to me. Shouldn't it be up to me to decide what happens to him?"

Mr. Anderson lowered his paper and peered at his daughter over the tops of his glasses.

"Don't sass your mother," he warned.

"I'm not sassing," Alice explained. "I'm asking."

"The last thing we need in this house is another mouth to feed," Alice's mother told her. "Polly may have found her little parting gift amusing, but I do not. Say your good-byes to the cat and have him ready to go at ten. Now where on earth could that rolling pin be?"

The toast popped up, but Alice wasn't hungry anymore. As her mother continued to dig through the kitchen drawers, Alice went to the cupboard and, unable to find any tuna fish, settled on a can of clam chowder instead. With a heavy heart, she carried it upstairs. Aunt Polly had always been so kind to her—how could Alice let her down by allowing Lardo to end up at the pound? If only she could think of some way to change her mother's mind!

In her room, Alice poured the clam chowder into the bowl and flopped down on her bed to wait. If Lardo was hungry enough, he might come out and eat his breakfast even though she was still in the room. After fifteen minutes, when she hadn't heard so much as a hiss out of him, Alice leaned over the side of the bed and, taking her life in her hands, carefully lifted the dust ruffle and peeked under. No Lardo. She quickly checked under the bureau, behind the desk, and in the closet. Still no Lardo. Alice had double-checked the door before she'd gone downstairs—she was sure of that—so the cat couldn't be anywhere else in the house, and that's when she noticed that the window was open.

"That's strange," she said to herself.

Alice was certain she had closed the window before she'd gone to bed. Her bedroom was on the second floor, and just outside the window was a beautiful old elm tree, whose branches grew so close to the house that on windy nights they sometimes rapped against the windowpanes like ghostly knuckles. Alice hurried across the room to close the window, but her heart sank when she saw the unmistakable mark of a cat's paw print on the sill.

She was too late. Lardo had escaped.

SOUR CHERRY PIE

4 cups pitted sour cherries
¾ cup sugar
3 TBS cornstarch

If it weren't for the pitting, this would be the
easiest pie on earth to make. Don't tell anyone I
said it, but canned cherries are a whole lot faster,
and the taste is actually not half bad. Place
ingredients in large saucepan and cook over medium
heat, stirring constantly until mixture comes to a
slow boil and thickens. Let cool for 10 minutes, then
pour mixture into piecrust, and cover with top crust.
If you've got the time to make a lattice, there's
nothing prettier than those red cherries peeking
out at you from between the cracks. Bake at 425 for
10 minutes, then lower temperature to 350 and cook
for 30 minutes more or until done.

Reminder: Reverend Flowers's favorite. (Birthday: May 11)

Chapter Five

"Mom!"

Alice came running down the stairs to report the news about Lardo, and found her mother standing in the hallway with a woman she didn't recognize.

"You're not going to believe this," Alice began breathlessly, but her mother put up a hand to stop her.

"Just a minute," she said. "Can't you see that I'm busy?"

"But, Mom, Lardo's—"

"Whatever it is will have to wait," Alice's mother told her. Then she turned back to the woman and said, "I'm sorry. What did you say your name was again?"

"Sylvia DeSoto. I'm a reporter with *LOOK* magazine. I was wondering if you might be willing to let me interview you for an article I'm writing about your sister."

Alice's mother sighed.

"Honestly," she said, "haven't you people written enough about Polly? What else could there be left to say?"

Sylvia DeSoto had on a flowered dress and high heels. Her yellow hair was piled up on her head like custard on a cone. She had a beauty mark on the right-hand corner of her upper lip and she wore thick horn-rimmed glasses that made her eyes look unnaturally large. Alice couldn't help thinking she looked like a goldfish peering out from inside a fishbowl.

"I'm particularly interested in the piecrust recipe," Miss DeSoto said, pulling out her notebook and flipping it open. "I understand she left it to her cat, but I was wondering if you could explain to me exactly *how* she did that?"

"Mom," Alice interrupted again, "there's something I really need to—"

"Not now, Alice," scolded her mother.

Miss DeSoto licked the tip of her pencil and looked at Alice's mother expectantly.

"You were saying?" she pressed. "About the recipe?"

"I have absolutely no idea why or how my sister did what she did with her recipe. For all I know, she whispered it in the cat's ear, or tattooed it on his belly, and frankly, Miss DeSoto, I don't care anymore," said Alice's mother. "Polly was a selfish woman, who did a selfish thing, and you can feel free to quote me on that. Now if you'll excuse me, I've got a pie to attend to."

Sylvia DeSoto raised an eyebrow.

"A pie?"

"My first," said Alice's mother. "It's a chocolate cream. My husband's favorite. Come back in September after I've won my Blueberry and I'll be happy to let you interview me about it."

Miss DeSoto looked shocked.

"*Your* Blueberry?" she asked.

"Well, someone's got to win it," said Alice's mother. "Why shouldn't it be me?"

"Forgive me, Mrs. Anderson, but the Blueberry is a rather lofty goal for an inexperienced baker such as yourself, don't you think? There are some who've waited *years* to be recognized."

Alice saw the color rise in her mother's cheeks.

"I may be inexperienced, Miss DeSoto, but I watched my sister make hundreds of pies and I don't see what all the fuss is about. You've heard the expression 'easy as pie'? Why do you suppose people say it?"

The shocked expression on Sylvia DeSoto's face dissolved into a sly smile.

"This wouldn't be your way of trying to tell me that you've got a little secret of your own, would it, Mrs. Anderson?" she asked.

"Whatever do you mean?" asked Alice's mother.

"You said you watched your sister make hundreds of pies — perhaps you know her recipe by heart, hmmmm?"

"You're barking up the wrong tree," said Alice's mother. "As I've told you, I don't know anything about my sister's piecrust recipe. According to my daughter, Polly never wrote it down. Perhaps you'd like to interview the cat. I believe you'll find him upstairs coughing up hair balls under Alice's bed."

"No, she won't," said Alice, unable to hold her tongue any longer. "Lardo ran away last night. That's what I've been trying to tell you, Mom. He's gone."

Alice's mother sighed again.

"My daughter has a flair for the dramatic," she explained to the reporter. "I'm sure the cat is just hiding somewhere. Now, Miss DeSoto, I don't mean to be rude but—" she stopped speaking midsentence and cocked her head to the side. "Forgive me for staring, but I just got the strangest feeling that we've met somewhere before. Your name doesn't ring a bell, but there's something very familiar to me about your face."

"Is there?" Miss DeSoto said, patting her hair nervously. "You must be mixing me up with someone else. I'm quite certain we've never met. In fact I'm *positive*. Now, don't let me take up even one more second of your valuable time. Best of luck finding your kitty cat, little girl, and best of luck winning that Blueberry, Mrs. Anderson. Trust me, you're going to need it!"

And just like that, she was out the door, leaving a wisp of flowery perfume behind her.

"What do you suppose she meant by that?" Alice's mother asked. *"'You're going to need it.'* That's rather rude, don't you think?"

"Shouldn't we go look for him?" Alice asked.

"Look for who?" her mother answered absently.

"Lardo, Mom."

"Look around the house. I'm sure he's just hiding somewhere."

"I did look. He's not here. Maybe we should put up some signs around the neighborhood in case somebody finds him."

"You do what you want," Alice's mother told her. "I have a pie to make."

It was obvious to Alice that her mother wasn't the least bit concerned about Lardo having run away, but her aunt Polly had trusted Alice to take care of him and she couldn't just let him wander around out in the world all by himself. What if he got sick? What if he starved to death or got hit by a car? Alice would never forgive herself.

"If I was Lardo, where would I go?" she asked herself.

The answer was so obvious, she felt silly for even having taken the time to ask the question. Two seconds later she was on her bike, pedaling off in the direction of the pie shop.

Alice hadn't been back to PIE since her aunt Polly had passed. Seeing the place without her aunt in it was not going to be easy, but PIE had been Lardo's home, too, so it seemed like the most logical place to start looking for him. The route she took happened to lead her past the Needlemans' house, where Alice caught sight of Nora jumping rope in the driveway by herself. She was pretty sure that Nora had seen her, too, but neither of the girls waved. Five minutes later, Alice arrived at the pie shop, and to her surprise she found the door standing wide open.

"Hello?" she called. "Is anybody here?"

Alice thought maybe she would find Reverend Flowers inside, since the pie shop belonged to him now, but when she stepped through the door, she gasped. The shop was a total wreck. Broken dishes and pans were strewn across the floor, the pie safes tipped over, their lovely hammered tin doors torn from the hinges. Everything had been knocked off the shelves, and when Alice looked in the pantry, it was even worse. Giant sacks of flour and sugar had been slashed open, and every basket and barrel overturned and dumped out.

A drop of sweat trickled down the back of her neck as Alice climbed the stairs up to Polly's apartment.

"Kitty, kitty, kitty?" she called nervously.

The door of the apartment was ajar, so Alice gently pushed it open with the toe of her shoe. It was almost noon and the sun streamed in through the windows, filling the place with a light so bright, Alice had to shield her eyes with her hand in order to be able to see. Blinking and squinting, she stepped into the apartment and nearly had a heart attack. Standing in the middle of the room was a tall figure in a dark cap, clutching a wooden baseball bat with both hands and winding up to take a swing at her head.

"No!" Alice shrieked, falling to her knees and covering her face with both hands.

She held her breath and waited for the end to come. When nothing happened, she inched two fingers apart and peeked out between them. Charlie Erdling was staring down at her, with his mouth hanging open.

"Good gravy, Alice," he said lowering the baseball bat, "you shouldn't creep up on a person that way. I almost beaned you."

Alice's terror did a fast U-turn and zoomed right past relief to anger.

"Are you nuts?" she shouted, jumping to her feet. "You could have killed me! And how dare you wreck Aunt Polly's pie shop after she was so good to you?"

"I didn't do it," Charlie insisted. "The place was like this when I got here. See, I was on my way to the ball field to fungo some baseballs when I noticed the door was open and stopped to close it. I saw the mess in the pie shop, so I grabbed my bat and snuck upstairs to see if I could catch him in the act."

"Catch who in the act?" Alice asked.

"The burglar," said Charlie. "Whoever did this came looking for something. You can tell by the way he tore the place up."

Alice looked around the room. Every cabinet and drawer had been yanked open and gone through. Even the cushions on the couch had been slit open and the stuffing pulled out. Charlie was right: Whoever had done this was clearly looking for something—but what? Aunt Polly had led a simple life and had very few possessions. The most valuable thing she owned was the piecrust recipe, and by now, everybody knew what had happened to that. The only things she cared about were people and pie and Lardo. And then it occurred to Alice—her aunt's Blueberry medals were made of gold. That must have been what the burglar was after!

She rushed into the bedroom and, sure enough, there was the cardboard box lying empty on the rug. What was strange, though, was that although the box was empty, the medals were still there, scattered haphazardly across the floor. Alice gathered them up and did a quick count. Thirteen. Not a single one was missing.

"I don't get it," she said, looking at the pile of shiny medals, each with its cluster of blueberries embossed on the front. "If the burglar wasn't after these, what could he have been looking for?"

"Maybe he was looking for a pie," said Charlie. "Your auntie sure did make some good ones. Did you ever taste her key lime? One bite of that pie and you'd swear you'd gone straight up to heaven. I sure am gonna miss it. Did you have a favorite, too?"

It seemed that everyone in Ipswitch had a pie they were going to miss more than any other, and Alice was no exception.

"Peach," she told Charlie.

Since Aunt Polly wouldn't have thought of using canned fruit, she had only made that pie for a few weeks during the summer when Pennsylvania peaches were at the height of ripeness. If you bit into one, the juice ran down your arm all the way to your elbow. Just thinking about the way that pie tasted made Alice want to cry.

"So what do you think? Was it pies he was after?" Charlie asked.

Alice shook her head. "Who would go looking for a pie under a bed?"

"Must have been some stranger from out of town," said Charlie. "Everyone around here knows that the only thing your auntie kept under her bed besides those medals was Lardo, and nobody in their right mind would want to tangle with him."

In the excitement of discovering the break-in and almost getting her head bashed in with a baseball bat, Alice had forgotten all about looking for Lardo.

"Have you seen him?" she asked Charlie. "He jumped out the window last night and ran away."

"I never saw Lardo jump," said Charlie. "Mostly he waddles."

Lardo was getting on in years, and his big belly tended to slow him down a bit.

"Okay, so maybe he *waddled* out the window," Alice said. "The point is, he's gone and I'm trying to find him."

"Did you examine the scene of the crime?" asked Charlie.

"What crime?"

"Oh, that's just something they say on *Sky King*. You ever watch that show? '*Out of the blue of the western sky comes Sky King!*'" Charlie said, imitating the deep voice of the announcer. Then he stuck his arms straight out from his sides and used his tongue to make a sound like the buzzing of an airplane motor.

Sky King happened to be one of Alice's all-time favorite television programs. The main character was a cattle rancher from Arizona who solved crimes on the side. He and his young niece, Penny, flew around chasing bad guys together in a little airplane called *Songbird*. Alice had actually been considering trying to grow out her hair that summer so that she'd be able to wear it in the same kind of ponytail Penny had. Alice was fine with the way she looked, but she wondered sometimes what it would feel like to be as pretty as a girl like Penny.

"Did you find any clues?" asked Charlie, letting his arms

drop back down by his sides. "Or did he vanish without a trace?"

Clearly, Alice wasn't the only one with a flair for the dramatic.

"I found a paw print on the windowsill in my room," she reported.

"Anything else?" Charlie asked.

Alice thought for a minute.

"I heard a noise," she said. "In the middle of the night. I thought maybe I dreamed it."

"What kind of a noise?"

Alice closed her eyes and tried to remember what she had heard.

"I think there were some thumps and I'm pretty sure there was a hiss," she said.

"Anything else?" asked Charlie.

"A *clink*," said Alice. "There was definitely a *clink*."

Charlie took off his cap and started scratching his head.

"A glass kind of *clink*, or a metal kind of *clink*?" he asked.

"Metal, I think."

"Interesting. Does Lardo wear a collar or a bell around his neck?"

"Nope."

"Do you have venetian blinds on your window, or a window shade with a metal pull on it?"

"Nope."

Charlie's eyes got very wide.

"Maybe it was aliens," he said. "Maybe they landed their tiny little metal spaceship on your windowsill, then they zapped Lardo with a shrinking ray gun and took him off to their planet to do scientific experiments on him."

"Are you serious?" asked Alice.

"Not really. But I did see a UFO once. Or at least I think I did. It might have been a cloud," said Charlie.

"What do you think Sky King would do if his cat ran away and the only clues he had to go on were some thumps, a hiss, and a *clink*?" Alice asked Charlie.

"I don't think Sky King has a cat," he said.

"That's not the point," Alice told him. "What I mean is, if Sky King was here right now, what do you think he would do?"

"I think he'd offer to come over to your house and try to help you figure out what made those sounds," said Charlie. Then he grinned and patted his stomach. "I also think he might wonder if you were going to offer him something for lunch when he got there."

"Do you like cream cheese and olive sandwiches?" Alice asked.

Charlie wrinkled his nose. "Got anything else?"

"Peanut butter and jelly."

"Now you're talking."

Alice had never invited a boy over to her house for lunch before, but if Charlie Erdling was willing to help her look for Lardo, the least she could do was give him a peanut butter and jelly sandwich.

"Let's go," she said, heading for the stairs.

Charlie hesitated.

"Shouldn't we call the police first?" he asked. "You know, to report the break-in?"

There was no phone in the pie shop anymore. Polly had decided to have it disconnected.

"Anyone who wants to talk to me is welcome to stop by the shop for a slice of pie and some chitchat," she always said.

"We can call the police from my house," Alice said.

Charlie hesitated again.

"Maybe we should bring your auntie's medals with us," he suggested. "In case the burglar changes his mind and decides to come back for them. They must be pretty valuable, being gold and all."

He had a point, so Alice gathered up the medals, put them back in the cardboard box, and carried it downstairs. They locked the door from the inside and pulled it closed. Then Charlie retrieved his bike from behind the pie shop, and the two of them headed off together toward Alice's house.

As it turned out, there was no need to call the police, because as Alice and Charlie rode past the parsonage, they saw Chief Decker sitting on the sunporch with Reverend

Flowers, drinking iced tea and shooting the breeze. Before the kids could even finish telling what had happened at the pie shop, the chief had jumped into his cruiser and raced off with the siren wailing.

Alice took the same route home, which meant that she and Charlie had to ride past the Needlemans' house.

"Hey, look," said Charlie, pointing. "There's Nora."

Nora had put away her jump rope and was lying on a blanket in the front yard, sunbathing in her bathing suit.

"So what?" said Alice.

"So nothing," Charlie responded.

Had Alice been paying attention, she would have seen that the tips of Charlie Erdling's ears had turned bright pink, but she was too busy thinking about Lardo to notice Charlie's ears, or the big green Chevrolet that was parked across the street from the Andersons' house when Charlie and Alice arrived.

HUCKLEBERRY PIE

4 cups fresh huckleberries (blueberries will do in a
pinch)
3 TBS quick-cooking tapioca
⅔ cup sugar
¼ cup apple juice
1 TBS lemon juice
2 TBS sweet butter

Rinse berries and let drain.
Add lemon juice.
Mix tapioca, apple juice, and sugar together.
Add sugar mixture to berries, toss with two forks,
and let stand for 15 minutes.
Pour as many berries as will fit into unbaked
pricked pie shell, dot with butter, and cover with
top crust, making sure to cut vents in top. Place a
cookie sheet or a piece of tin foil under the pie.
Nothing's harder to clean off an oven than burnt
huckleberry pie. Doesn't smell great, either!
Bake at 450 for 10 minutes, then reduce heat to 350
and bake another 40-45 minutes more.

*Reminder: Elsie and Herb Decker both love this pie. (Wedding
anniversary: June 15)*

Chapter Six

"Anybody home?" Alice called as she and Charlie walked in the door.

There was no answer. Charlie tipped his head back and sniffed.

"What is *that*?" he asked. "Smells like something burning."

It didn't take long to find the source of the unpleasant odor.

"Good gravy," said Charlie.

Sitting on the kitchen counter was the ugliest pie Alice had ever seen in her life. The whole thing was lopsided, the edges of the crust burnt to a crisp, and in the middle was a pool of pale brown liquid with several lumps of what appeared to be butter floating in it like pale yellow icebergs.

"What is that supposed to be?" Charlie asked.

"I think it's a chocolate cream pie," said Alice.

"It doesn't look like any chocolate cream pie I ever saw."

"That's because my mom's never made a pie before," Alice explained. "She's decided she's going to try to win the Blueberry Award this year."

"You better tell her to get in line," said Charlie.

"What do you mean?"

"I deliver groceries to practically every house in town, and I can tell you that ever since your auntie passed, there's been an awful lot of pie baking going on around here."

Charlie wasn't exaggerating. At that very moment, there were forty-seven pies baking in various ovens around Ipswitch.

"Do you think they're all trying to win the Blueberry?" asked Alice.

"Maybe. I heard Mrs. Ogden say something about it, and Pete Gillespie, too."

"Pete Gillespie from the gas station?"

Charlie nodded.

"He had me deliver a ten-pound bag of yams and a gallon of corn syrup yesterday. If his sweet potato pie brings home the Blueberry, he says he's going to move to Florida so he can go fishing all day and never have to fix another flat tire for as long as he lives."

Alice wondered if her mother was aware that she wasn't the only one in town who'd come down with a bad case of Blueberry Fever.

"Besides Mrs. Ogden and Pete Gillespie, who else do you know who's planning to enter a pie in the contest?"

"My mom was planning to take a shot at it," said Charlie. "But she changed her mind. Yesterday she tried to make a gooseberry pie and it came out so bad, even the dog wouldn't touch it. And he drinks out of the john!"

"Maybe this year it won't be someone from Ipswitch who wins," said Alice. "People from all over the country send in their pies."

"Judging from what I've seen so far, the only one in this town who's got a chance of winning is Lardo."

"Lardo?"

"I'm just kidding," said Charlie. "You know, because your auntie left him the piecrust recipe. Why did she do that, anyway?"

"That's what everybody keeps asking, but it's a mystery," Alice told him. "*The Mystery of the Secret Piecrust Recipe* sounds like a Nancy Drew book, doesn't it?"

"How would I know? Those are for *girls*," Charlie scoffed.

"What about the Hardy Boys? You must have read one of those."

Charlie blushed and looked down at his feet.

"To be honest," he said, "I'm kind of bad at reading. Spelling, too. I get things all mixed up."

Alice looked at the pie sitting on the counter. The Blueberry committee would be making the announcement in only a few short weeks. Her mother had her heart set on winning, but unless some kind of miracle occurred there was no way that was ever going to happen.

"You ready to eat?" she asked Charlie.

"Always," he answered.

Alice got out the peanut butter and jelly, and she and Charlie made sandwiches for themselves. As they ate their lunches sitting across from each other at the kitchen table, Alice found herself thinking about how much she was going to miss having lunch with Aunt Polly at the pie shop. At twelve o'clock on the dot, Polly would turn off the oven and hang the PLEASE COME BACK LATER sign on the door. Upstairs, they'd eat cream cheese and olive sandwiches, and afterward Polly would cut them each a big slice of pie. Alice wasn't allowed to have dessert after lunch at home, but Aunt Polly had her own rules, one of which was that a little pie never hurt anybody.

"Your auntie sure was a nice lady," said Charlie. "You must really miss her."

It was almost as if he could tell what Alice was thinking.

"It's going to get even worse when August comes," she told Charlie.

"How come?"

"Peaches," Alice said, biting her lip.

"Oh, right," said Charlie. "Your favorite pie."

Alice nodded and wondered if there would ever come a time when she wouldn't miss her aunt Polly so much it hurt.

• • •

When they had finished eating, Alice asked Charlie if he wanted something for dessert. Just because she wasn't allowed to have any didn't mean he couldn't. Charlie glanced nervously at the chocolate cream pie on the counter.

"Don't worry," Alice told him, opening the cupboard and taking out a bag of Chiparoons. "We've got cookies, too."

"*Reach for Nabisco,*" Charlie started to sing. "*Reach for Nabisco.*"

Nabisco was one of the commercial sponsors on *Sky King.* Alice knew the jingle by heart, too, so she sang the rest of it along with him.

"*The bright red seal on the package end means mighty good cookies inside, my friend.*"

Charlie grinned at her and pulled a cookie out of the bag.

"Did you ever notice that *package end* and *my friend* is a perfect rhyme?" Alice asked.

"Nope," said Charlie. "But I've noticed that Chiparoons taste good." He shoved the whole cookie in his mouth and reached for another.

After they had finished cleaning up from lunch, Alice led Charlie upstairs.

"I just thought of something funny," Charlie said. "Instead of visiting the scene of the crime, we're about to visit the scene of the *clink*."

Alice didn't think it was that funny, but she laughed anyway so Charlie wouldn't feel bad. As a rule, she didn't like boys very much, but she had to admit, Charlie was actually pretty nice. As they headed down the hall on the way to her room, Charlie tilted his head back and started sniffing the air again.

"Did your mom by any chance make *another pie*?" he asked.

This time the offending odor was not the result of a pie gone wrong. Alice had forgotten to throw away the clam chowder she'd put down for Lardo that morning.

"Be right back," she told Charlie.

When Alice returned after disposing of the chowder, Charlie was in her room, examining the windowsill.

"The thumps you heard were probably made by Lardo trying to get up on the windowsill. The hiss, well, that's a no-brainer, since Lardo hisses at pretty much anything that moves," Charlie said. "But that *clink* has me stumped. You're sure he wasn't wearing a collar?"

"Positive," said Alice.

She bent down to scratch a mosquito bite on her ankle, and when she did, something caught her eye. She began crawling on her hands and knees toward the window.

"What are you doing?" asked Charlie.

"I see something shiny," Alice said. "Under the radiator."

Charlie crouched down beside Alice as she reached under the radiator and ran her hand along the floorboards until her fingers found what they were looking for. She had thought maybe it was a broken shoe buckle or a bottle cap that had rolled under the radiator somehow, but when she pulled it out, she was surprised to discover that the shiny metal object that had caught her eye was an earring.

"Is it yours?" asked Charlie.

Alice shook her head. She wasn't allowed to wear earrings yet.

"Is it your mom's?"

Alice shook her head again. Her mother wore earrings sometimes when she got dressed up — she even owned a pair of gold hoops that looked a lot like the one Alice had just found, except that her mother's earrings were clip-ons. This earring was the kind of hoop you had to have pierced ears to be able to wear.

"Maybe some lady who lived in the house before your family moved in dropped the earring on the floor a long time ago, and you just didn't find it until now," said Charlie.

"Look at my hand," Alice said.

"What about it?"

"There's no dust on it at all. I vacuum under the radiator every time I clean my room, so I would have found it by now."

"Then how do you think it got there?" asked Charlie.

That's when Alice realized what it was she was holding in her hand.

"This must be the *clink*!" she cried.

"I thought you said you heard it in the middle of the night," said Charlie.

"I did."

"Other than Santa Claus, who comes to visit people in the middle of the night?"

Alice's heart began to race.

"Maybe it wasn't a visitor," she said excitedly. "Maybe it was a catnapper!"

"A *what*?"

"A catnapper. She must have crawled up the tree and opened the window from the outside — then she grabbed Lardo, and on the way out she dropped her earring, *clink*."

"You think it was a *woman*?" asked Charlie.

"How else do you explain the earring?"

"Pirates wear earrings," said Charlie defensively.

Alice gave him a look.

"Okay, fine," he said. "It probably wasn't a pirate. But who in their right mind would sneak into somebody's house in the middle of the night to steal a grumpy old cat?"

"I don't know," Alice said. "But Sky King and Penny always say you should trust your hunches, and I have a hunch that somebody crawled in my window last night and took Lardo and that whoever it was, was wearing this earring. And you know what else? I bet it's the same person who broke into the pie shop."

"But why?" asked Charlie.

"I don't know," said Alice. "But I'm sure if we put our heads together, we can figure it out."

A car door slammed outside, and a minute later Alice heard her father calling.

"Alice! Come down here, would you, please? It's important."

"I'd better go see what he wants," she said. "Come on."

Charlie followed Alice down the stairs and into the living room, where Mr. and Mrs. Anderson were waiting.

"Hello, Charlie," said Alice's father.

"Hello, Mr. Anderson. Mrs. Anderson," said Charlie politely.

"I'm glad you're both here. I understand you two were the ones who discovered the break-in at the pie shop," said Mr. Anderson.

"Yes, sir," said Charlie.

Alice was surprised. "How did you know about that?" she asked her father.

"Chief Decker called and told us to meet him down at the station," Alice's mother said. "He wanted to talk to us about the key."

"What key?" Alice asked.

"It was all a big mix-up," her father explained. "The lock on the pie shop didn't appear to have been tampered with, so the police were convinced that whoever broke in used a key to open the door."

"Until I explained to them why that was impossible," said Alice's mother. "There was only one copy of the key, and Polly was wearing it on a chain around her neck when she was buried."

"No, she wasn't," Alice said, suddenly realizing what it was that had seemed wrong about Polly when she'd looked at her at the funeral. She hadn't been wearing the chain with the key on it!

"I saw it with my own two eyes, Alice," her mother said.

"You couldn't have seen the key," said Alice. "It wasn't there."

"Don't sass your mother," Alice's father warned.

"I'm not sassing," Alice told him. "I know for a fact that Aunt Polly wasn't wearing that key around her neck when she was buried."

"And I know for a fact that she was," her mother insisted. "The pie shop was unlocked when Mr. Ogden went to pick up Lardo. He assumed someone had a key, so he locked the door from the inside, and pulled it closed when he left. Or so he says."

"The break-in happened sometime between then and when you two arrived," said Alice's father.

"So the obvious explanation is that Mr. Ogden didn't lock the door properly," her mother finished.

"But that still doesn't explain why Aunt Polly wasn't wearing the —"

Alice's father gave Alice a stern look, so she let the matter drop.

"I suppose you know your aunt's Blueberry medals were stolen," Alice's father said. "The police are dusting the place for fingerprints right now."

Before Alice could even open her mouth to explain that she and Charlie had brought the medals home with them, her mother took off on one of her rants.

"If you ask me, it's all Mayor Needleman's fault," she said. "He's been so busy campaigning for reelection he hasn't been doing the job he was elected to do in the first place. He ought to be beefing up the police force to protect us from crimes like this. Instead he's been kissing babies and shaking hands and posing for every photographer that pushy wife of his can manage to shove him in front of."

"The medals weren't stolen, Mom," Alice said, when her mother finally paused to take a breath. "They're in a box outside in the basket of my bike."

"It was my idea," Charlie explained. "I thought it would be safer than leaving them in the shop. I guess we should have told Chief Decker."

"The police recovered a baseball bat they think the burglar might have used during the crime," said Mr. Anderson. "You wouldn't know anything about that, would you, Charlie?"

Charlie turned a shade of red Alice had never seen a person turn before. "It's mine," he admitted sheepishly. "I must have left it behind by accident."

"What a colossal waste of time this day has turned out to be!" Alice's mother said, collapsing in a chair. "Bring me some aspirin, George. I feel another headache coming on."

Alice's father went off to get the aspirin, and her mother closed her eyes and began rubbing the bridge of her nose.

"Maybe I ought to get going," Charlie said.

"Now?" asked Alice.

"Well, I promised Miss Gurke I'd pick up a few things for her at the store this afternoon. I've got the list right here." He patted his back pocket. "She told me to get there by five. She gets really frosted if I show up late."

"You can't leave now," Alice told Charlie. "You have to help me figure out who catnapped Lardo."

Alice's mother opened one eye.

"Did you just say what I think you said?"

Alice swallowed hard.

"I know you're probably going to think I just imagined this, Mom, but I'm absolutely positive that somebody crawled in my window in the middle of the night last night and stole Lardo. And whoever it was, dropped this." Alice held up the earring.

"George!" cried Mrs. Anderson. "What's taking you so long? I need that aspirin *right now.*"

"And one more thing," Alice said. "I have a hunch it's the same person who broke into the pie shop."

"Enough!" barked Alice's mother. "If I hear one more word about keys or cats or cockamamie ideas about people climbing through windows, wearing gold earrings, I promise you my head is going to jump right off my neck and fly around this room like a bald eagle."

Alice's father arrived with the aspirin and shooed Alice and Charlie out of the room. Charlie seemed relieved.

"I'd better get going," he told Alice again. "Thanks for lunch. And good luck finding Lardo."

"What do you mean, 'good luck'?" Alice asked. "I thought you were going to help me."

Charlie began shifting his weight from one foot to the other.

"I'm awful busy," he said, looking down at his shoes. "And, like I said, Miss Gurke is waiting. . . ."

"Did anyone ever tell you that you're a terrible liar, Charlie Erdling?"

"I'm not lying," he said. "I really do have a delivery to make. I'll show you the shopping list if you don't believe me."

"Don't bother. I get the message," Alice said. "You don't think Lardo's been catnapped, do you?"

Charlie looked down at the ground.

"Probably not," he said softly.

"Fine. Then I don't want your help anyway," Alice told

him. "The last thing I need is somebody else who thinks my imagination is too active."

"Aww, don't be sore, Alice," said Charlie.

"Don't tell me how to be," Alice snapped. "I'm fine just the way I am, which is more than I can say for you."

"What's that supposed to mean?" asked Charlie.

"Figure it out for yourself," said Alice. "Oh, I forgot, your brain doesn't work right. Maybe you better ask your little girlfriend, Nora, to help you figure it out."

Charlie frowned and threw one long leg over the crossbar of his bike. Before he left, he looked Alice straight in the eye.

"I may not be the smartest guy in the world," he told her, "but I'll tell you one thing I know: Your aunt Polly never would have talked to a person the way you just talked to me. And she wouldn't have thought very highly of somebody who did, either."

Without another word, he pushed off, rolled down the driveway, and rode away.

CHOCOLATE CREAM PIE

1 cup sugar
3 TBS cornstarch
2 TBS cocoa powder
pinch of salt
3 cups milk
3 egg yolks
1 tsp vanilla
1 TBS butter

In a saucepan, combine the sugar, cornstarch, cocoa powder, and salt.
In a separate bowl, beat egg yolks and milk. Add to saucepan and blend.
Cook over medium heat, stirring constantly until mixture thickens. Remove from heat.

Stir in vanilla and butter. Pour into baked pie shell. Cool. Refrigerate. Serve with whipped cream.

Reminder: George's favorite. (Birthday: February 9)

Chapter Seven

After Charlie left, Alice went and sat on the porch steps. Hugging her knees tightly to her chest, she closed her eyes as a wave of sadness washed over her. Nothing was right with the world anymore. Her aunt Polly was gone, her mother was annoyed, and now Charlie was mad at her, too. She shouldn't have said what she'd said to him, but what was she supposed to do? Lardo had been catnapped, she was sure of it, and nobody would even listen to her. Aunt Polly had always listened. Alice remembered a time years ago when her aunt had asked her what she wanted to be when she grew up. Alice had said that more than anything in the world, she wanted to be a squirrel. Most people would have laughed, but Polly didn't. Instead she told Alice that she would make sure to leave plenty of walnuts out on the porch during the winter months so that Alice wouldn't have to dig around in the snow when she got hungry.

Alice didn't even realize that she was crying until she felt a teardrop fall on her bare leg. With her eyes still closed she began to sing—

Who's going to leave me walnuts?
Who's going to make me pie?
Who's going to love me as I am?
Why did you have to die?

"Ah-hem . . . ah-*hem*."

It took a minute for it to register that the sound Alice had heard was someone clearing his throat. Lifting her head, she was mortified to discover Charlie Erdling standing at the bottom of the steps, staring up at her.

"What are you doing here?" Alice asked, swiping at her hot tears with the back of her hand.

"I lost my shopping list," Charlie said. "It must have fallen out of my pocket. Do you mind if I look around to see if I dropped it here?"

"Go ahead," Alice said, too embarrassed to even look at him. It was bad enough that she'd been mean to him, but she could only imagine what he must think of her now that he'd heard her singing to herself about walnuts. Part of her wanted to explain, but most of her wanted to crawl under a rock and hide.

Charlie quickly retraced his steps, but he didn't find the shopping list.

"Oh, well," he said. "Hopefully, Miss Gurke won't kill me if I can't remember everything."

He started to leave, but Alice stopped him. She could almost feel her aunt Polly's hand on the small of her back, pushing her to step forward and say what needed to be said.

"I'm sorry," Alice told Charlie. "For the crummy thing I said about your brain. I won't blame you if you decide to hate my guts forever."

"I don't hate your guts," said Charlie. "I know I'm no genius, but I can't help the way I am."

"There's nothing wrong with the way you are," Alice said. "Aunt Polly was the smartest person I've ever known and she always used to say, 'That Charlie Erdling has a good head on his shoulders.'"

"Yeah?"

Alice could tell that Charlie was pleased.

"And I was only teasing about Nora," she added. "Who would want to have a stuck-up person like that for a girlfriend anyway, right?"

"Right," said Charlie. "I mean, good gravy, just 'cause she looks like Penny from *Sky King* doesn't mean I want to marry her or anything, you know?"

Alice felt a little twinge of something she couldn't quite identify.

"You really think Nora Needleman looks like Penny?" she asked.

"Yeah," said Charlie. "But so would you if your hair was a little longer."

Alice could have kissed him right then and there for saying that, except that the idea of kissing Charlie Erdling, or any other boy for that matter, made her want to throw up.

"Good luck with Miss Gurke," she said.

"Thanks," said Charlie, and he got on his bike and rode off again toward the A&P, only this time he turned around and waved before he sailed around the corner and out of sight.

It was not long after this that Alice noticed the folded-up piece of paper wedged between two boards of the porch step she had been sitting on. It was Charlie's shopping list. Alice unfolded it and began to read what he had written.

1 Box BANd-AydES
1 cAN vEgtiblE shortNiNg
1 BAg sANd

The handwriting was terrible, and Charlie hadn't been kidding when he'd said that he wasn't very good at spelling.

Alice started to refold the paper when the fourth and final item on the list caught her eye.

1 duzzin cans Sardeens

Suddenly everything fell into place, and Alice knew for sure that her hunch had been right.

• • •

Charlie was just leaving the A&P when Alice arrived, breathless from having ridden her bike like the wind to catch up with him.

"What are you doing here?" Charlie asked when he saw her.

Alice was panting so hard she couldn't speak, so she handed Charlie the shopping list.

"Gee," he said, "it sure was nice of you to come all this way to bring it to me."

He unfolded the paper and ran his finger down the items on the list.

"Let me see, I remembered to get the Band-Aids and I remembered to get the vegetable shortening. Drat, I forgot all about the sand. It's too late to go to the hardware store now. I'll have to do it tomorrow."

"What about the sardines?" Alice asked, having finally caught her breath.

"Got 'em," said Charlie, holding up the paper bag of groceries.

"No, I mean *what about the sardines?*" she said.

"What about them?" Charlie asked.

"Who do you know who likes sardines?"

"Obviously, Miss Gurke does," said Charlie. "Otherwise, why would she want twelve cans of them?"

"Good question," Alice said. "And you know what I think? I think the reason Miss Gurke needs all those sardines is because she's the one who catnapped Lardo."

"*Miss Gurke?*" said Charlie incredulously.

"The clues are all right there on the shopping list," Alice told him, and she began ticking things off on her fingers. "She needs sand for his litter box, and the Band-Aids are for the scratches Lardo probably gave her when she snatched him."

"What about the vegetable shortening?" asked Charlie. "What's that supposed to be for?"

"That's the most important clue of all," Alice told him. "The reason she needs vegetable shortening is because she's making a pie."

Charlie scratched his head.

"Why would Miss Gurke have to steal your auntie's cat if she wants to make a pie? Everybody and their uncle has been making pies around here lately, and none of them had to steal a cat to do it."

"It's not the cat she needs — it's the piecrust recipe. That's what she was looking for when she broke into the pie shop, but she didn't find it. So the next day, when *The Ipsy News* ran the story about Aunt Polly leaving the recipe to Lardo, she decided to catnap him."

"Wait a minute. Back up," said Charlie. "You think Miss Gurke was the one who broke into the pie shop?"

"I don't *think* so — I *know* so," said Alice. "I saw her steal the key."

"When?"

"At the funeral. She reached into Aunt Polly's casket and then she jerked her hand back out real quick. I didn't realize it at the time, but she must have taken the key."

"Don't get mad," said Charlie, "but your mom said she saw the key."

"That's because she *did* see the key. It was there when *she* looked at Aunt Polly, but by the time *I* looked at her, Miss Gurke had already stolen it."

"Good gravy," said Charlie. "Are you sure?"

"Come on," Alice said. "I'll prove it."

Even though Charlie was not completely convinced, he allowed Alice to talk him into letting her follow him to Miss Gurke's house. On the way, her bicycle chain slipped off and the pedals began to spin around without catching hold. Charlie heard the clattering and circled back around to help.

Watching him work with the greasy chain, Alice understood why his fingernails looked the way they did.

"What if Miss Gurke catches us snooping around?" Charlie asked nervously. "She might get really steamed."

"Don't worry," said Alice. "She's not going to catch us."

• • •

When they got to Miss Gurke's house, they found her car parked in the driveway. It was clear from the dripping garden hose and the bucket of soapy water standing beside it that it had recently been washed. The big green car gleamed like a lizard basking in the sun. Charlie and Alice stashed their bikes in the bushes.

"Are you scared?" asked Charlie. "I mean, you've heard the stories, right?"

There were a lot of rumors that had been passed around school over the years about Miss Gurke and the reason she wore such loose-fitting clothes. One of the most popular stories was that she was hiding the mummified body of a kid who'd been tardy to school one too many times. Alice tried not to think about that as she dove headfirst into a bank of holly that ran along the front of Miss Gurke's house. A minute later, Charlie joined her.

"*Next time, let's pick a bush without prickers,*" he whispered, wincing as he pulled off a spiky holly leaf that was stuck to one of his palms. "*What do we do now?*"

"Let's peek in the window. If we see any sign of Lardo, we'll go straight to the police," Alice whispered back.

There was a big picture window in the front of Miss Gurke's house. Charlie and Alice crawled on their bellies, commando-style, across the lawn until they were situated just beneath it.

"Ready?" asked Alice.

Charlie nodded and slowly they rose up until their noses were resting on the sill.

"See anything?" Alice whispered, peering through the glass into Miss Gurke's living room.

"Just some furniture," said Charlie.

thwack . . . thwack . . . thwack

Charlie and Alice froze.

"What was that?" Charlie whispered.

thwack . . . thwack . . . thwack

The sound seemed to be coming from the backyard. Alice signaled Charlie to get down, and they crawled across the lawn and around the corner to the back of the house.

THWACK . . . THWACK . . . THWACK

It was louder now, and in between the thwacks was another sound, like a little grunt.

The backyard was surrounded by a wooden fence that was too high to see over. Charlie put one finger to his lips, warning Alice to be quiet. Then he squatted down and inter-laced his fingers to make a little basket. Alice slipped her foot into his hands and Charlie boosted her up.

THWACK . . . grunt . . . THWACK . . . grunt . . . THWACK . . .
grunt . . .

"*What is it?*" Charlie called up to Alice. "*What do you see?*"

There was only one word Alice could think of to describe the terrifying sight that lay on the other side of that fence, and her voice was shaking so badly she had trouble getting it out—

"Muh-muh-muh," she stammered.

Just then, Charlie heard a buzzing sound near his left ear. A giant horsefly was circling his head. Anyone who's ever been bitten by a horsefly knows that it's an experience worth avoiding if at all possible, but when Charlie felt the fly land on the back of his neck, he wasn't able to swat it, because his hands were busy holding on to Alice's foot. When the fly bit him, Charlie yelped and jumped three feet in the air, letting go of Alice's foot with such force that it launched her over the fence like a missile straight into Miss Gurke's backyard.

"What on earth!" Miss Gurke sputtered as Alice landed at her feet in a heap. "Were you *spying* on me?"

It's hard to imagine many things more unsettling than seeing your principal without her clothes on. Not that Miss Gurke was naked—thank goodness—but the bright red, skintight outfit she was wearing that day was a far cry from the kind of clothing she normally wore. Even more shocking than the outfit itself was the fact that Alice now knew what

Miss Gurke had been hiding under her loose clothes. *Muscles.* Great big ones. Standing there in her skimpy red suit, Miss Gurke didn't look like a principal at all, she looked like Charles Atlas, the beefy muscleman Alice had seen pictures of in magazine ads. From her bulging biceps to her rippling calves, Miss Gurke's rock-hard body glistened in the sunlight like a glazed ham. No wonder she'd been able to tear the pie shop apart. She was *huge.*

"What do you have to say for yourself?" demanded Miss Gurke.

Alice was speechless. She had come there to accuse Miss Gurke of catnapping Lardo, but looking at those giant muscles, all she could think about was Aunt Polly's couch cushions with all the stuffing yanked out. Alice hoped she wasn't about to meet the same fate as those poor pillows.

"Well?" said Miss Gurke. "Let's have it."

Ding-dong. The doorbell chimed from inside the house, and Alice breathed a huge sigh of relief. Whoever it was, Alice would explain everything to them. The police would come and take Miss Gurke off to jail. Then Alice would bring Lardo home and spend the rest of her life trying to forget the horrifying sight of Miss Gurke in that stretchy red outfit.

"Don't move," Miss Gurke told Alice. Then she reached for her robe, which was hanging over the back of a chair, slipped it on, and went to answer the door.

A minute later, Alice heard Charlie's voice coming from inside the house.

"HERE YOU GO, MISS GURKE," he shouted. "I GOT THE GROCERIES YOU ASKED FOR."

"Put the bag on the table over there," Miss Gurke instructed. "And there's no need to shout, young man. I'm not deaf."

Charlie wasn't shouting for Miss Gurke's benefit; he was trying to let Alice know that he hadn't abandoned her. After all, it was his fault that she'd ended up on the wrong side of the fence.

"IS EVERYTHING OKAY?" Charlie shouted. "DON'T BE SHY. SPEAK RIGHT UP."

Alice wanted to run inside or call out to Charlie to get the police, but she was afraid it would make Miss Gurke even madder.

"I don't know what's gotten into you today, Charles," said Miss Gurke. "You're certainly behaving strangely."

"MAY I JUST SAY, THAT IS A VERY LOVELY ROBE YOU'RE WEARING TODAY, MISS GURKE," Charlie shouted. "THE COLOR REALLY BRINGS OUT THE BLUE IN YOUR EYES. AND THE MATERIAL IS SO, WELL, NUBBY, I THINK WOULD BE A GOOD WORD TO DESCRIBE IT, DON'T YOU?"

Alice couldn't imagine why Charlie was babbling on about Miss Gurke's bathrobe until it dawned on her that he might be trying to distract Miss Gurke to give Alice time to escape. Sky King himself would have been proud of that plan! Looking around for something to stand on, Alice spied a folding aluminum lawn chair and quickly dragged it over to the fence. But when she climbed up on it, her feet immediately slipped through the plastic webbing and the chair toppled over, taking Alice along with it and making a terrible clatter in the process.

"DID I MENTION THAT I FORGOT TO BRING THE SAND?" Charlie asked, shouting even louder now in an attempt to try to cover up the racket Alice was making.

"What on earth is the matter with you?" Miss Gurke cried.

Charlie was running out of ideas. So he decided it was time to come clean.

"I didn't mean to do it, Miss Gurke," he said. "A horsefly bit my neck, and the next thing I knew, Alice was flying over your fence."

"Oh," said Miss Gurke. "So you and your little girlfriend were in cahoots?"

"I don't know what 'cahoots' means, and Alice is not my girlfriend, but I'm the one who threw her over the fence, so if you're going to turn one of us into a mummy, it ought to be me."

Alice, who was still hopelessly tangled up in the chair, was beginning to panic. Nobody knew where she was and clearly the police weren't on the way. Charlie had done his best, but now it was time for her to step up to the plate, so she did the only thing she could think of to do—she screamed.

The minute Miss Gurke heard Alice screaming, she raced for the door with Charlie at her heels. As they barreled out of the house into the backyard, visions of mummies and violated couch cushions flashed before Alice's eyes and she screamed even louder. Miss Gurke bounded down the steps, reaching for Alice with her massive arms, but the belt of her robe got caught on the door handle, yanking her backward like a dog on a leash. When she tried to pull herself free, the robe fell open, revealing her gigantic muscles to Charlie for the first time. His eyes practically popped out of their sockets as he took in the sight of Miss Gurke in her skimpy red suit. Then a strange sensation came over him, like somebody popped a Fizzie into his head and carbonated his brain.

"Good gravy, Miss Gurke!" said Charlie. "You look exactly like—"

But before he could finish his sentence, everything went black.

LEMON CHESS PIE

4 eggs
1½ cups sugar
3 TBS cornmeal
¼ cup sweet butter, melted
½ cup whole milk
2 lemons, juiced

Combine eggs, sugar, cornmeal, melted butter, milk,
and lemon juice in a large bowl.
Mix until sugar is dissolved, but do not beat. Pour
filling into unbaked pricked pie shell.
Bake at 425 for 10 minutes. Reduce temperature to
350 and continue to bake until set. Cornmeal will
form a crust on top of custard. This is the very
best part, so if you don't have cornmeal in the
pantry — borrow some from a neighbor or make some
other kind of pie! Cool before serving.

Note: Lucille Gurski's favorite. (Birthday: April 15)

Chapter Eight

Charlie lay crumpled on the ground. Alice, who had finally managed to untangle herself from the chair, ran to him.

"He'll be fine," said Miss Gurke, who was squatting down beside him, fanning Charlie's face with her hand. "He's fainted."

Charlie groaned and opened his eyes.

"What happened?" he mumbled.

"You fainted," Alice told him. "When you saw—"

She glanced nervously at Miss Gurke.

"Oh, yeah," said Charlie, sitting up and rubbing his head. "Now I remember. I was just about to tell Miss Gurke she looks exactly like—"

"Miss America," said Alice, quickly jumping in.

"No," said Charlie. "I was going to say she looks like—"

"*Miss America,*" Alice insisted. She wasn't about to let Charlie tell Miss Gurke that she looked like Charles Atlas, or a raging buffalo, or whatever else he'd been about to say. They were in enough trouble as it was without adding fuel to the fire.

"Do you really think Miss Gurke looks like Miss America?" Charlie asked Alice.

"Yes," said Alice, exasperated with Charlie for being so slow to catch on. "I really do."

"*Really?* Miss America?"

"Stop saying that," growled Miss Gurke.

"It's supposed to be a compliment," said Alice. "Miss America is a beauty queen."

Miss Gurke jumped up and strode across the lawn to a canvas laundry bag that was hanging on a chain suspended from the branch of a tree.

"I know who Miss America is. Do you think I've put myself through hours of hard training to become some mindless *beauty queen?*" she asked as she balled up her glistening fists and began punching the bag.

thwack . . . grunt . . .

"Beauty pageants are insulting to women."

. . . thwack . . . grunt . . .

"Little girls need better role models."

. . . thwack . . . grunt . . .

"Women who aren't afraid to say to the world . . . 'READY OR NOT, HERE I COME!'"

. . . *thwick, thwick, thwick, thwick* . . .

She pummeled the bag with a final barrage of rapid-fire punches. Then, dropping her fists, she turned and struck a pose, her powerful arms curling up at her sides like giant cobras.

"Does this look like the body of a woman who should be spending her days making sure that lazy, ungrateful little children aren't late for school?" she asked. "Well, *does it*?"

"No, ma'am," Charlie and Alice answered in heartfelt unison.

"That's right," said Miss Gurke through gritted teeth. "Which is why I'm not about to let two nosy little whipper-snappers spoil my dream of becoming America's first muscle woman by spilling the beans before I'm ready."

"We don't want to spoil your dream," Charlie said. "And we won't spill the beans about your muscles."

"Just give Lardo back," said Alice, "and we won't say a word."

Miss Gurke broke her pose.

"Lardo?" she asked.

"There's no use pretending you don't have him," said Alice. "I found your earring under the radiator."

"What in the world are you talking about?"

"You're the catnapper," Alice said. "And you're the burglar, too. I have proof."

"Proof of what?" asked Miss Gurke, and Alice had to admit she was doing a very convincing job of pretending she didn't know what Alice was talking about.

"It's all on the shopping list. How else do you explain the Band-Aids and the sand and the sardines?" Alice asked.

"Not that it's any of your business, but I use sand to fill my punching bag, and Band-Aids to protect my knuckles. As for the sardines, they're high in protein, which is essential for maintaining muscle mass. Is there anything else you'd like to know?"

Alice knew it was time to play her ace.

"Why did you reach into Aunt Polly's casket?" she demanded.

Miss Gurke looked shocked.

"You saw that?" she asked, the color draining from her face.

"Yes," said Alice triumphantly. "I saw you take the key. Sorry, Miss Gurke, but *the jig is up*."

It was an expression Penny and Sky King used when they cornered a bad guy, but instead of caving in and admitting her guilt, Miss Gurke looked even more confused.

"What key?" she asked. "I dropped my ring in the casket."

Miss Gurke reached into the pocket of her robe and took out the diamond ring Alice had noticed her wearing on the day of the funeral. "It's the vegetable shortening," Miss Gurke explained to Alice. "It's great for tanning, but it makes you slippery." She slipped the ring onto her right ring finger and tipped her hand to the side to demonstrate how easily it could have slid off. "I didn't mean any disrespect to your aunt, Alice, but this ring belonged to my late mother. So when it fell into the casket, I couldn't just leave it behind."

Alice felt like a balloon with a hole poked in it, the air leaking out with an embarrassing sound. All of the clues that had pointed so clearly to Miss Gurke seemed ridiculous now.

"Maybe we should get going," Charlie said, pushing Alice toward the door. "Sorry to have bothered you, Miss Gurke. I'll bring you that bag of sand tomorrow, okay? No charge."

"Not so fast," said Miss Gurke. "We're not finished here."

Ten minutes later, Charlie and Alice rode away on their bikes, but not before they had struck a deal with Miss Gurke that they would keep her muscles a secret. In return she wouldn't report them to the police for trespassing in her backyard.

"I'll ride home with you if you want," Charlie told Alice. "In case your chain comes off again."

"That's okay," she said. "You don't have to."

But he did it anyway.

Alice was embarrassed that she had falsely accused Miss Gurke and she felt awful about getting Charlie in trouble. Her aunt Polly had been wrong—having an active imagination wasn't a good thing at all.

They had only gone a couple of blocks when Alice's chain came flying off again.

"Maybe tomorrow you should bring your bike over to my house," Charlie suggested. "I've got my tools there, so I could fix it for good."

"You want me to come over to your house?" asked Alice.

"Sure," said Charlie. "If you want to."

"Why aren't you mad at me?" Alice asked, as Charlie went to work fixing the chain.

"I don't know," said Charlie. "I guess I don't like the way it feels."

"I'd rather be mad than sad," said Alice.

"I'd rather be happy," Charlie said.

Alice didn't say it, but she wondered if she'd ever feel happy again. When the chain was back in place, she and Charlie got back on their bikes and continued on in silence.

"It's going to get better, you know," Charlie said after a while.

"What is?" asked Alice.

"The missing."

"Aunt Polly was my best friend," said Alice. "I'm never going to stop missing her."

"That's how it was with me and my grandma," said Charlie. "She died three years ago and I didn't think I could stand it, I missed her so much. But then I came up with this little trick."

"What kind of trick?" asked Alice.

Charlie hesitated. "Promise you won't make fun of me?"

Alice didn't blame him for not trusting her.

"I promise," she said.

"I keep one of her old perfume bottles in my drawer. When I really miss her, I close my eyes and take a sniff and it feels like she's right there in the room with me."

"Aunt Polly didn't wear perfume," said Alice.

"That's too bad," said Charlie.

After that they didn't talk for a while. Alice was feeling lower than low. No wonder her mother was so annoyed with her all the time. She probably wished she had a different kind of daughter, a girl more like Nora Needleman, who would want to dress up with her in matching hats. Instead she was stuck with a daughter who made up dumb songs and ran around accusing innocent people of being catnappers. Alice felt a sad song coming on, but she pushed it away. She'd already made a big enough fool of herself in front of Charlie for one day.

As they biked through town Alice noticed a number of houses with pies cooling out on the windowsills. Was that all anybody in Ipswitch cared about anymore? Winning the Blueberry? Alice would have traded a million Blueberry Awards for a chance to spend one more day in the pie shop with Aunt Polly.

As she and Charlie turned the corner and headed up the block toward the Andersons' house, Alice was surprised to see a police car parked in the driveway.

"Uh-oh," said Charlie. "Looks like maybe Miss Gurke changed her mind and decided to tell on us after all."

"You go ahead home," Alice told him. "The whole thing was my fault anyway. You only went along with it because I made you."

But Charlie insisted on coming in with her.

"I'm the one who pitched you over the fence," he pointed out.

Alice's parents were in the living room, sitting next to each other on the couch. Chief Decker was standing behind them with his hand resting on his holster, and sitting on the coffee table was a cardboard box, the top closed with masking tape.

"It's about time," said Alice's mother when Alice and Charlie walked in. "Where on earth have you been?"

Apparently, Miss Gurke hadn't reported them after all.

"Alice was keeping me company while I made a delivery," Charlie said. "To Miss Gurke."

It was the truth, but with a number of important (and embarrassing) details left out.

Alice saw her parents exchange a look.

"What is it?" she asked.

"It's Lardo," said her father. "I'm sorry, honey, but I'm afraid he's—ahh-ahh—"

"Dead?" asked Alice, fearing that her horrible day was about to become even worse.

"—*choo!*" Her father sneezed. "No, no, not dead."

"Then what?" asked Alice.

"See for yourself," Alice's mother said, pointing to the cardboard box. "But I warn you, he's not himself."

Alice heard a muffled hiss coming from inside the box.

"He *sounds* like himself," she said.

"Dick Kaperfew found him wandering around outside the Ipsy Inn, recognized him, and called it in," Chief Decker explained. "I put him in that box so he wouldn't scratch me."

"Don't think this changes anything, Alice," her mother told her. "Regardless of what's happened, he's still going to the pound in the morning."

Alice bent over the box and began pulling off the tape. The minute the flaps came loose, Lardo scrambled out and tumbled off the edge of the coffee table onto the floor. Alice's mother had not been exaggerating when she'd said that he was not himself.

Lardo's yellow eyes were glazed over and completely crossed. He struggled to his feet and stood swaying back and forth like a sailor on the deck of a rocking ship.

"Good gravy!" cried Charlie. *"He's drunk!"*

KEY LIME PIE

1 14-oz can sweetened condensed milk
2 large egg yolks
½ cup fresh lime juice
3 egg whites at room temperature
¼ tsp cream of tartar
6 TBS sugar
½ tsp vanilla
1 prebaked graham-cracker crust (9 inch)

1) Preheat oven to 350.
2) Mix together condensed milk, egg yolks, and lime juice. Blend well and pour mixture into piecrust.
3) Beat egg whites together with cream of tartar until soft peaks form. Gradually add vanilla and sugar, beating until stiff. Spread mixture over pie. I use a table knife or the back of a soupspoon to shape meringue into peaks.
4) Raise oven rack a notch and bake for 12-15 minutes until tips of meringue peaks are lightly browned.
5) Allow pie to cool to room temperature. Refrigerate until chilled.

Reminder: Charlie Erdling loves this pie and can easily eat a whole one without any help! (Birthday: December 30)

Chapter Nine

Chief Decker shook his head.

"If it was alcohol, we would be able to smell it on him," he said. "My guess is that the cat's had himself a dose of sleeping powder."

"*Sleeping powder*? Where would Lardo find that?" asked Alice.

"As I explained to your folks," Chief Decker said, "either he dug around in someone's garbage and accidentally ate some, or else it was kids playing a prank. Teenagers get bored in the summer and come up with all kinds of crazy ways to amuse themselves."

"That's how my dad's tractor ended up on the roof of the barn last summer," said Charlie.

"Exactly." Chief Decker chuckled as he put the finishing touches on his report and handed a copy to Alice's father.

Alice hoped that when she became a teenager she would have better things to do than give sleeping powder to a cat or put somebody's tractor on the roof.

Lardo hiccupped twice, then made his way unsteadily across the room, weaving and stumbling up the stairs to Alice's room.

"Is he going to be okay?" Alice asked.

"I'm sure he'll be fine by morning," Chief Decker told her. "He just needs to sleep it off. I will say I'm mighty relieved I won't be spending my night trying to chase down a dangerous catnapper."

He looked at Alice and winked. Obviously, her mother had told him about her catnapping theory. Great. One more person to add to the list of people who thought she was completely nuts.

"Tell her about the pie shop, Herb," said Alice's mother. "So we can put that ridiculous notion to rest as well."

"Since there was nothing stolen, I suspect the break-in boils down to the same thing as the cat," Chief Decker told Alice. "Kids looking for a thrill. I'm glad to know your aunt's medals are safe, though. Would have been a shame to lose all those Blueberries. They're an important part of this town's history."

"Speaking of Blueberries," said Alice's mother, "can I offer you fellas a slice of pie, before you go? It's chocolate cream."

"Homemade?" asked Chief Decker.

"Very much so," said Alice's father under his breath.

"Did you make it, Alice? I know how you loved spending time at the pie shop."

"I don't know how to bake a pie," said Alice. "Mom made it."

"How about you?" Mrs. Anderson asked Charlie. "Would you like a piece, too?"

"Oh, no, thank you," said Charlie quickly. He remembered that pie all too well. "It's almost dinnertime and I wouldn't want to spoil my appetite."

"Nonsense. A growing boy like you? Run and get it out of the fridge, Alice. And bring a couple of plates and forks."

Charlie looked absolutely mortified, but Alice had no choice but to do as she'd been told and fetch the pie from the kitchen. On the way, she overheard her mother proudly telling Chief Decker that if she had anything to say about it, Ipswitch wasn't finished making Blueberry history yet.

"You sound like my Elsie," Chief Decker told Alice's mother. "She's been talking my ear off about winning the Blueberry herself this year. Can you beat that? Don't get me wrong, my Elsie's a fine woman, but she doesn't have your sister's gift for pie baking."

"So Elsie's been baking pies, too, has she?" asked Alice's father.

"To the tune of three or four a day. I've got the heart-burn to prove it." Chief Decker pounded his chest with a fist and winced. "I love my wife, but she's no Polly Portman. Don't tell her, Ruth, but I've got half of one of your sister's huckleberry pies hidden in the freezer at home. I picked it up at the shop the day before she passed, but I can't bear to eat it."

Alice thought of the slice of lemon chiffon pie she'd eaten the night before, and wished that she had thought to freeze it. Had she known what was going to happen, she would have filled the freezer with enough of Aunt Polly's pies to last a lifetime.

"As long as it's there," Chief Decker continued, "I don't have to face the thought that I might never taste a Polly Portman pie again."

"Perish the thought," said Alice's mother sarcastically. Then she called out to the kitchen, "Alice! What's keeping you with that pie?"

Chief Decker looked at his watch. "I'm afraid I'm going to have to take a rain check. I didn't realize it was so late. Elsie's probably already got supper waiting on the table." Then he turned to Charlie and said, "Run and grab your bike, son. We'll toss it in the trunk of the cruiser and I'll give you a lift home."

Charlie raced for the door, relieved to have escaped without being forced to taste the chocolate cream pie.

"Tell Alice I said good-bye," he called over his shoulder as he ran out.

As soon as they were gone, Ruth Anderson snatched up the newspaper, which had been lying open on the couch, and furiously crumpled it into a ball.

"Hey, I wasn't finished reading that yet," her husband started to protest, but when he saw the look in his wife's eyes, he stopped.

"Here's a news flash for you, George," she told him. "Elsie Decker's trying to steal the Blueberry right out from under me."

"Now, Ruthie, don't get yourself in a twist. You heard what Herb said—Elsie doesn't have Polly's gift. I'm sure her pies are no better than yours are."

"Well, if that isn't a backhanded compliment, I don't know what is."

"Mom!" Alice called from the kitchen. "Can you come out here, please?"

Alice's mother stuffed the balled-up newspaper into the trash basket and went out to the kitchen.

"What is it?" she asked.

"I can't find the pie," Alice told her.

"It's in the refrigerator," said her mother.

"No, it's not."

"I put it there myself, Alice."

"Well, it's not there anymore," Alice said.

"Don't sass your mother," Alice's father warned as he joined them in the kitchen.

"I'm not sassing," said Alice. "I've looked everywhere and the pie's not here."

"Don't be ridiculous," said her mother. "Of course it is."

But a thorough search of the kitchen confirmed what Alice had said: The pie was nowhere to be found.

"That's odd," said Alice's father. "I had the exact same experience today with my shoes, and I still haven't figured out where they are."

"If you're talking about your black wing tips, George, I stuck them in a box out on the curb this morning for the Salvation Army to pick up."

"You gave away my shoes?"

"You said they pinched."

"They did," said Alice's father. "But other than that, they were perfectly good."

"Can we get back to my pie, please?" said Alice's mother. "Tell the truth, George. Did you eat it?"

"Absolutely not," he told her. "I haven't seen that pie since this morning."

"Well, it didn't just grow legs and walk out of here on its own, " said Alice's mother. "So where is it?"

The thought occurred to Alice that maybe her father had thrown the pie away and didn't want to admit it. Or maybe Elsie Decker or Pete Gillespie had stolen the pie to eliminate their competition for the Blueberry Award. Alice shook her head. What was the matter with her? Hadn't she learned her lesson? The last thing she needed to do was try to solve another mystery.

"I have no idea what happened to your pie, Mom," said Alice. "I'm going upstairs to check on Lardo. Call me when it's time to set the table."

Alice's mother announced that she was in no mood to cook that night, so it was decided that the Anderson family would have dinner downtown at the diner instead.

"You go ahead," Alice told her parents. "I'm not hungry."

The truth was, Alice didn't feel right about leaving Lardo alone, especially if it was going to be their last night together. She found a carton of cream in the refrigerator, poured some in a little bowl for Lardo, and carried it upstairs. She expected to find him hiding under the bed but instead discovered him lying on his back in the middle of the rug, snoring loudly.

Alice kicked off her shoes and curled up on her bed. She tried not to think about all the awful things that had happened that day. She tried not to think about the mean thing she'd said to Charlie about his brain. She tried not to think about accusing Miss Gurke of being a catnapping burglar. She tried not to think about how she'd left the window open and it was all her fault that Lardo had ended up eating sleeping powder, and most of all, she tried not to think about how disappointed her aunt Polly would be in her right now.

Alice felt a song coming on and as darkness fell she sang it softly to herself.

If I could make a wish right now
I know what I would do.
I'd wish to be some other girl
And hope it would come true.

Alice had trouble sleeping that night. She had an awful dream. Everywhere she looked she saw pies. Perfect pies, with tender crusts, overflowing with every imaginable kind of delectable filling. How delicious they all looked and smelled! Her mouth watered 'til she felt she couldn't bear another second without having a taste, but each time she reached for a pie, just as she was about to touch it, the pie would vanish into thin air. She woke up whimpering into her pillow.

"I'd rather be happy," Charlie had told her.

But happiness seemed as far from Alice's reach as the disappearing pies in her dream. She lay in bed wondering if things would ever change, and that's when she remembered something her aunt Polly had once told her.

"Things do not change; we do."

"Did you make that up?" Alice had asked.

"No, a man named Henry David Thoreau said it. Do you understand what it means?"

"I'm not sure."

"If you want things to be different, you have to start by changing yourself."

• • •

The next morning when Alice got up, Lardo was still sound asleep on the rug, but at some point during the night he had drunk the cream and, even better, used the litter box properly. Alice smiled. Maybe she wasn't the only one who was ready to make some changes. It was a beautiful, sunny day and Alice couldn't wait to get downstairs to introduce her mother to the new and improved version of Alice Anderson.

She had made herself a promise: From this day forward, things were going to be different because *she* was going to be different. The new Alice wasn't going to make up annoying little songs and sing them to herself, and she wasn't going to have ridiculous hunches, and most important of all she was never, ever going to let her imagination run away with her again. As she folded her pajamas and tucked them under her pillow, a happy song began to form in Alice's head, but she caught herself just in the nick of time. It would take some getting used to, but she was determined to keep her promise: no more songs, no more hunches, no more active imagination.

Mrs. Anderson was in the kitchen, frying bacon, when Alice came downstairs. Her father, as usual, was reading the newspaper.

"Good morning," Alice said cheerfully.

"G'morning," mumbled her father without looking up.

"What are you in such a good mood about?" asked her mother over the sound of sizzling bacon.

"I was thinking maybe we could go shopping together today, Mom," Alice said. "For hats."

Alice's mother turned to look at her.

"Hats?"

Alice nodded.

"Nora Needleman and her mother have matching hats," she said. "And I thought it might be nice if we had them, too. So we could be alike."

Alice's father had lowered his paper and was staring at her.

"What's gotten into you?" he asked.

"Nothing," said Alice. "I just thought it might be nice for Mom and me to spend some time together. We don't have to buy hats. We could just stay home and talk instead."

"About what?" asked Mrs. Anderson, turning back to her bacon and adjusting the flame.

"Whatever you want," said Alice. "Aunt Polly and I did that all the time. She'd tell me what was on her mind, and then I'd tell her what was on mine, and before you knew it, we'd chatted away the whole day."

"In case you haven't noticed, your aunt Polly and I are nothing alike," said Alice's mother. "She may have had the luxury to sit around and chat all day, but I don't. Especially not now."

"A little shopping might do you good, Ruthie," said Alice's father. "Get your mind off this whole Blueberry thing."

"Oh, is that how it's going to be now, George? The two of you ganging up on me? Well, I won't have it. I'm going to get myself a new rolling pin today—and I'm going to make another pie, even better than the last one. I've spent my whole life living in Polly's shadow, but those days are over now."

"If you say so, dear," said Alice's father, returning to his newspaper.

"I could help you, Mom," Alice said. After all, she'd helped Polly plenty of times in the pie shop. Even though she'd never made a pie herself, she *did* know a few things about how it was done.

Alice's mother turned and looked at her.

"You took it, didn't you?" she said.

"Took what?" asked Alice.

"My pie. That's why you're being so nice to me this morning. Look at her face, George. There's guilt written all over it."

"She looks the same as she always has to me," said Alice's father, peering at his daughter over the tops of his glasses.

"I didn't take your pie, Mom," said Alice. "Why would I do that?"

"Because you're just like your aunt Polly, that's why. Two peas in a pod. You don't want me to succeed any more than she did."

This was not going at all the way Alice had planned. She had pictured her mother smiling at her, as they tried on their matching hats together in front of the mirror. Instead her mother was accusing her of being a liar and a thief as the smell of burning bacon filled the kitchen.

Alice's mother went on. "Polly took everything from me. Even you. From the time you were a baby, you'd light up at the sight of her, reach out your little hands to her. It broke my heart, but that didn't stop her. What Polly wanted, Polly got. All those hours you two spent together in the pie shop—she knew exactly what she was doing. She had to make sure you loved her more than me, and clearly she succeeded."

"You're wrong," Alice told her mother, fighting to hold back the tears that had sprung to her eyes. "I didn't love Aunt Polly more than I love you. The difference is she loved me back."

Alice turned and ran out of the room, out of the house, down the steps, and out to the garage, tears streaming down her face. How could she have been so stupid to think that she could change herself or the way that her mother felt about her?

"*Alice!*" she heard her mother calling. "*Come back.*"

But Alice didn't want to go back. Ever. She got on her bike and began to pedal. She didn't know where she was going, and she didn't care. She just needed to get away. Away from the mother who couldn't love her, away from the pain of missing her aunt Polly, away from a kitchen that would never, ever smell like freshly baked pie, away from everything.

"Alice!" her mother called again.

But Alice just kept riding. Away, away, away.

CONCORD GRAPE PIE

5 cups Concord grapes
2 apples, peeled
¾ cup sugar
½ cup flour

Wash grapes and pinch off the skins, reserving the
skins for later. Heat grape pulp, boiling for about
5 minutes. Put through strainer to remove seeds.
Use enough grape skins to layer pie shell (unbaked).
Slice up apples to cover grape skin layer. Mix
sugar with flour. Sprinkle half of mixture over
skins, pour cooled pulp into shell, and add remaining
flour and sugar mixture. Cover with top crust. Bake
at 425 for 20 minutes. Reduce heat to 350 and bake
25 minutes more.

Helpful hint: To pinch off grape skins without
bruising the fruit, squeeze gently between thumb
and forefinger — kind of like shooting a watermelon
seed.

Guess whose favorite this one is? Mine!

Chapter Ten

The Ipsy Inn was on the top of a hill overlooking the town of Ipswitch. Alice usually avoided that area when she was out riding her bike. The hill was too steep to ride up, and she didn't want to have to walk her bike all the way to the top. But that day, Alice hadn't been paying attention to where she was going and when she found herself at the bottom of the hill, she decided to try to make it to the top. At first it wasn't so hard, but before long, Alice found she had to stand up on her pedals in order to keep the bike moving forward. The hot sun beat down on her as she struggled inch by inch to push herself up the hill. Her chest burned and her back ached but she refused to give up, and five minutes later, with one final push, she reached the top — just as her bicycle chain slipped off.

Alice left her bike at the curb while she went and flopped down in the grass to catch her breath. She closed her eyes and lay on her back, listening to the steady pounding of her heart. After a while she opened her eyes again and looked across the yard at the inn. It was a beautiful old white clapboard house with black shutters and a bright red door. Snowball hydrangeas were in full bloom along the front, and in the side yard there were crisp white bedsheets hanging on a clothesline, billowing and snapping in the warm breeze. A little yellow bird flew by, landing on the edge of the roof, then fluttering down to perch on a pot of geraniums hanging on a hook outside one of the second-floor windows. Alice saw someone moving inside, and then the window swung open, startling the little bird away.

Shielding her eyes with one hand, Alice watched as a woman leaned out the window. It was Sylvia DeSoto, the reporter. She wasn't wearing her glasses, but Alice recognized her from her yellow hair, which was piled up on her head exactly as it had been the day she'd come to the Andersons' house. As Alice watched, Sylvia DeSoto leaned out the window a little farther and looked both ways, then she ducked back inside, reappearing a few seconds later holding something in her hands. Even from a distance, Alice could tell that it was her mother's chocolate cream pie. Miss DeSoto looked both ways again, then dropped the pie, tin pan and all, out of the window into the bushes below.

"Good gravy!"

Alice practically jumped out of her skin. She'd been so wrapped up in watching Sylvia DeSoto, she hadn't heard Charlie arrive. He was standing right behind her, straddling his bike and looking up at the window of the inn.

"Did you see what I saw?" he asked.

Just then the front door opened and Sylvia DeSoto walked out carrying a brown leather suitcase in her hand.

"Quick!" Alice told Charlie. "Look busy."

Charlie squatted down beside Alice's bike and started fiddling with the chain while Alice pretended to be helping him.

"What's she doing now?" he whispered.

"She's walking over to her car," Alice reported, glancing over her shoulder. "Wait. No, she's stopping. She's turning around and going back into the inn. She must have forgotten something."

"Like a chocolate cream pie?" said Charlie.

"Wait. She's stopping again. Now she's digging around in her purse looking for something. Oh, her glasses."

As Alice watched, Miss DeSoto slipped on her glasses, then she picked up her suitcase again and carried it over to a green Chevrolet that was parked in the corner under the shade of a shagbark hickory tree. After putting the suitcase in the backseat, she climbed into the front and started the engine.

"We have to follow her," said Alice.

"Why?" asked Charlie.

"My mother's never going to believe me if I tell her I found her pie in the bushes," said Alice. "She thinks I took it, and she always will if we don't catch Miss DeSoto and get her to admit what she did."

"Who's Miss DeSoto?" asked Charlie. "And what's she doing with your mother's pie?"

"I'll explain later. We have to go now before we lose her."

"We can't go," said Charlie. "Or at least you can't."

"Why not?" asked Alice, her eyes still glued to the green car, which was pulling out into the street now with the right-turn indicator blinking.

"Your chain is totally busted," said Charlie. "I can't fix it without my tools."

"It doesn't matter," said Alice. "Everything is downhill from here — I can coast. Come on. Hurry up before she gets away."

Two seconds later, they were sailing down the steep hill in pursuit of the big green Chevrolet. Alice had promised herself that she would never let her imagination run away with her again, but she hadn't imagined that pie flying out the window, had she? Near the bottom of the hill, Miss DeSoto turned left, and left again at the next corner. Alice would not be able to go much farther without being able to pedal.

"Where do you think she's going?" she asked Charlie.

As if in answer to her question, the brake lights flashed red up ahead and the green Chevrolet slowed down and came to a stop at the end of the Needlemans' driveway.

"Welcome, welcome!" Mrs. Needleman gushed, rushing out of the house to greet her guest. "Henry and I are so glad you could make it. He's waiting inside for you in the den, Miss DeSoto."

Charlie and Alice had cut through the neighbor's yard and were hiding behind some trash cans, listening in.

"I'm glad you called," said Miss DeSoto, as she climbed out of her car and shook hands with the mayor's wife. "I had just about given up hope."

Melanie Needleman had heard through the grapevine that a reporter from *Look* magazine had come to town sniffing around for information about Polly Portman's piecrust recipe. Never one to turn down an opportunity for publicity, especially during an election year, she had called over to the Ipsy Inn and stretched the truth a little by suggesting that the mayor had somehow managed to find a copy of the recipe, which he might be willing to share if Miss DeSoto would be so kind as to interview him for the article she was writing.

"I'm most eager to speak with your husband," Miss DeSoto told Mrs. Needleman. "I simply must have that recipe before it's too late — to write the article, I mean."

"Yes, yes, the piecrust recipe," said Mrs. Needleman with a wave of her hand. "That's all anyone seems to care about anymore. Come inside, Miss DeSoto. I'll make us all a nice cup of tea, and you and Henry can chat. I had hoped to have some homemade buttermilk pie to offer you, but I'm afraid it didn't turn out very well. Have I mentioned that the mayor is running for reelection? He's got some very interesting ideas you might be able to use in your article. . . ."

Charlie and Alice couldn't hear the rest of the conversation as Mrs. Needleman led the reporter inside.

"Now what?" asked Charlie.

Alice looked at the green Chevrolet.

"You stay here and be my lookout," she said. "If you see anyone coming, whistle."

"I can't whistle," Charlie told her. "I don't know how."

"Then make some other kind of sound," said Alice. "Just cover me, okay?" She scooted down the driveway and slipped into Miss DeSoto's car.

The first thing Alice saw was a black hat with a veil lying on the passenger seat. That wasn't very incriminating, but her luck improved when she opened the glove compartment. There she discovered a white handkerchief with something wrapped up inside it. Alice carefully unfolded the little square of linen and smiled. It was a gold hoop earring, exactly like the one she'd found under the radiator.

"I knew it!" she whispered.

Somewhere nearby, a cat began to meow. Alice ignored it and continued her search, but when the meowing grew louder, she suddenly realized it wasn't a cat at all; it was Charlie trying to warn her that someone was coming. Alice dove into the backseat, held her breath, and waited. Pretty soon she heard a high singsongy voice.

Cinderella
Dressed in yella
Went upstairs to kiss a fella . . .

It was Nora Needleman reciting a rhyme as she jumped rope.

By mistake she kissed a snake
How many doctors did it take?
One, two, three, four . . .

Alice waited what seemed like an eternity for Nora to finish jumping and go back inside. When she was sure the coast was clear, Alice climbed out of the car and hurried back to Charlie.

"Look what I found," she said, holding out the gold earring.

"Hey, that looks just like the one you—"

"It is," said Alice excitedly. "And that's not all. Her suitcase has the initials *J.Q.* engraved on it."

Alice had discovered this while she was hiding in the backseat of the car.

"Why would somebody named *Sylvia DeSoto* have a suitcase with the initials *J.Q.* on it?"

"Because she's not Sylvia DeSoto—she's somebody else!" said Alice. "Somebody who's come here looking for Aunt Polly's piecrust recipe. That's why she broke into the pie shop and it's the reason she stole Lardo, too."

"Don't kill me for saying this," said Charlie, "but this new hunch of yours sounds an awful lot like the old hunch you had about Miss Gurke. And you remember how *that* turned out."

"I know," Alice told him. "But this time I'm right."

"Why do you think she threw your mother's pie out the window?" asked Charlie.

"To get rid of the evidence."

"Why did she steal it in the first place?" Charlie asked.

Alice explained that Miss DeSoto had seemed very interested in her mother's pie, *too* interested in fact, and that she'd probably stolen it because she wanted to see if Alice's mother was telling the truth when she said she didn't know the recipe by heart.

"So you think Miss DeSoto was the one who gave Lardo the sleeping powder, too?" asked Charlie.

"Yes," said Alice.

"Why would she do that?"

"I don't know. But one thing I'm sure of is she's after that piecrust recipe, and you're about to make her think she's going to get it."

"I am?" asked Charlie.

Alice nodded. "I've got a plan all worked out."

"What do you want me to do?" Charlie asked. "Spy on her or something? I think I might be pretty good at that."

"No. I want you to invite Nora to go to the movies with you," Alice said.

"What?" cried Charlie. *"Are you crazy?"*

"Shh!!" Alice said, pressing a finger to her lips.

"I am *not* asking Nora Needleman to go to the movies," Charlie said. "Besides, she wouldn't go with me even if I did ask her. I'm pretty sure she hates me."

"She hates me more," Alice said. "But it's the best excuse I can think of for why you would have to come over to her house to talk to her."

"Why do I have to talk to her in person?" asked Charlie. "Can't I just call her on the phone?"

"No," Alice said.

"Why not?"

"I need you to be overheard."

Alice quickly explained the plan to Charlie, who listened carefully and reluctantly agreed to follow her instructions.

"When do I have to do it?" he asked.

"Right now."

"Good gravy," Charlie grumbled as he climbed the front steps and rang the doorbell. Mayor Needleman answered the door.

"What can I do for you, young man?" he said with a friendly smile.

"Is Nora at home, sir?" Charlie asked, his voice cracking and jumping an octave, he was so nervous. "I need to speak to her about a personal matter."

"Nora!" the mayor called over his shoulder. "There's someone here to see you, honey." He turned back to Charlie. "What's your name, son?"

"Charlie Erdling."

"Dorothy and Ed's boy?" asked the mayor.

Charlie nodded.

As Alice watched from her hiding place behind the trash cans, she saw Nora Needleman appear at the door with a bottle of pink nail polish in her hand. Fluffy white cotton balls peeked out from between each of her toes, and she was walking tipped back on her heels in order to keep from smudging her freshly painted toenails.

"What do *you* want?" she asked when she saw Charlie.

"I was wondering if we could talk," Charlie said.

"About what?"

"POLLY PORTMAN'S PIECRUST RECIPE," shouted Charlie.

The mayor's eyebrows shot up.

"Polly Portman's piecrust recipe?" he said. "What a coincidence. We were just talking about that inside."

"Really? You were just talking about POLLY PORTMAN'S PIECRUST RECIPE?" Charlie shouted again.

"Why are you shouting?" asked Nora.

"Was I?" said Charlie. "I didn't mean to."

"What on earth is going on out there, Henry?" Mrs. Needleman called from the den.

"There's a young man here who's come to talk to Nora about—"

"POLLY PORTMAN'S PIECRUST RECIPE," Charlie shouted, finishing the sentence for him.

Alice couldn't have been more pleased. Charlie was following her instructions perfectly.

"I don't see what Polly Portman's piecrust recipe has to do with me," said Nora. "And for golly's sake, quit shouting, will you?"

"Mind your manners, Nora," said her father. "Why don't you invite the young man to sit in the porch swing with you while I go inside and finish my interview."

"Henry!" called Mrs. Needleman. "We're waiting. *Look* magazine is waiting."

"Coming, Melly," said the mayor.

Hobbling on her heels, Nora led Charlie over to the porch swing.

"Sit," she told him.

Alice saw the curtain move as the window behind Charlie slid open a crack. *So far, so good*, she thought.

"Did you really come all the way over here to talk to me about piecrust?" asked Nora. She hadn't joined Charlie in the swing, choosing instead to stand in front of him, with her arms crossed.

Charlie pulled at his collar, and even from a distance, Alice could see that the tips of his ears were bright red.

"I was wondering if you'd like to go to the movies with me this Saturday," he said.

"*What?*" said Nora, her mouth dropping open.

"I said, I was wondering if you'd like to go to the movies with me this Saturday," Charlie repeated.

"What does going to the movies have to do with piecrust?" asked Nora.

Charlie took a deep breath. *Here we go*, Alice thought.

"I WAS GOING TO ASK ALICE ANDERSON TO GO TO THE MOVIES WITH ME, BUT NOW THAT SHE'S FOUND HER AUNT POLLY'S SECRET PIECRUST RECIPE, SHE DOESN'T HAVE TIME FOR THINGS LIKE GOING TO THE MOVIES ANYMORE."

"You're shouting again," said Nora.

"I just want to make sure you heard me when I said that ALICE SURE HAS CHANGED SINCE SHE FOUND THAT RECIPE. ALL SHE TALKS ABOUT NOW IS HOW RICH SHE'S GOING TO BE WHEN SHE SELLS IT. SHE EVEN SLEEPS WITH IT UNDER HER PILLOW EVERY NIGHT. CAN YOU BELIEVE IT? RIGHT UNDER HER PILLOW."

"Charlie Erdling," Nora said, stamping her foot so hard, several of the cotton balls popped out from between her toes, "I always knew you were strange, but I had no idea you were *this* strange. Do you really think I would consider going to the movies with someone like you?"

Charlie took another deep breath.

"LIKE I SAID, I WOULD HAVE ASKED ALICE, BUT NOW THAT SHE FOUND THAT PIECRUST RECIPE —"

Alice whistled long and low three times — the signal she and Charlie had agreed she would give as soon as she felt he'd accomplished his mission. He heard Alice and wrapped things up quickly.

"Well, Nora," he said, "it sure has been nice chatting with you. I'm sorry about all the shouting and, no, I didn't really think you'd go to the movies with me, but when it comes to asking beautiful girls to the movies, all I can say is you can't blame a guy for trying."

Alice hadn't told him to say that, especially not the part about Nora being beautiful. But otherwise, Charlie had done everything exactly the way she'd asked him to. All that was left to do now was wait for the rat to take the bait.

```
                    PECAN PIE

3 eggs, beaten
1 cup brown sugar
1 TBS butter, softened
1 cup light corn syrup
1 cup pecans, chopped, plus 6-8 pecan halves for
the top
1 tsp vanilla
¼ tsp salt
```

Cream butter and sugar, add syrup and well-beaten
eggs, salt, and vanilla, mix well, and add pecans.
Pour into unbaked pie shell. Line the top with
pecan halves. Bake for 1 hour at 325.

Suggestion: Serve with hard sauce instead of
whipped cream or, better yet, homemade honey ice
cream.

*Reminder: Thanksgiving dinner at the parsonage goes on the
table at 4:00 p.m. Three pies ought to do the trick.*

Chapter Eleven

Alice couldn't stop thinking about the plan.

"What if Sylvia DeSoto, or whoever she is, doesn't take the bait? What if she leaves town?" Alice asked Charlie. "No one's ever going to believe me."

She had walked her bike over to the Erdlings' house so that Charlie could fix her chain once and for all.

"I believe you," said Charlie.

"Hey, you two!" Mrs. Erdling called out to them. "Lunch is on."

Having skipped breakfast that morning, Alice was starved. Mrs. Erdling made franks and beans. Charlie bolted down four hot dogs in about two seconds flat. Alice only had one, but she could have eaten another if there had been any left.

"When you're finished, you've got a whole slew of messages waiting for you," Charlie's mother told him. "Mrs.

Ogden called three times. She's got a long list of things she wants you to pick up, including a can of black shoe polish for her husband's dress shoes."

"It's almost two o'clock already. I'm never going to be able to make all of these deliveries today," Charlie said, sorting through the pile of messages.

"Maybe I could help," suggested Alice. "I go grocery shopping with my mom all the time."

"Really? You wouldn't mind?"

"It'll be a good distraction. I'm going to go out of my gourd if I sit around all day worrying about whether my plan is going to work."

So the two of them hopped on their bikes and headed off to the A&P.

"Okay," said Charlie, handing Alice half of the shopping lists. "You get this stuff and I'll get the rest. Meet me at the checkout counter when you're finished."

Alice began wheeling her shopping cart up and down the aisles collecting the items on her lists. Three bags of sugar for Reverend Flowers, two dozen eggs for Mrs. Decker, a bag of unsweetened coconut for Mrs. Kaperfew, and a bunch of ripe bananas for Mr. Evans. Mrs. Ogden's shopping list was the longest of all, and when Alice had located every-thing — including a can of black shoe polish — she headed for the checkout counter at the front of the store. Charlie was already standing in line, a giant sack of yams balanced on his shoulder.

"Find everything okay, you two?" asked the cashier as she began to ring things up.

"Everything but buttermilk," Charlie told her.

"The mayor's wife must have cleaned us out. She was in here yesterday and bought three cartons."

Charlie plopped the bag of yams down on the counter.

"Don't tell me these are for Pete Gillespie. Didn't you just take him a bag? What on earth is that man doing with all these sweet potatoes?"

"He's trying to get to Florida," Charlie explained.

After the groceries had been bagged and paid for, the next step was to figure out how to pack everything into the bike baskets. Charlie handed Alice a carton of eggs.

"You better take these," he told her. "I'm not very good with breakables."

"You may not be good with eggs, but you sure are good with bike chains," said Alice, as they pedaled along. "Mine hasn't slipped off once since you fixed it."

"When I grow up I'd like to have my own bike shop," Charlie said.

"You could call it Spokes for Folks," Alice suggested. "Or Deals for Wheels."

"I was thinking of calling it Erdling's," said Charlie.

"That's good, too."

Rather than splitting up, Alice and Charlie decided to make the deliveries together.

"We can share the tips," Charlie offered.

But Alice didn't want any money; she was happy to help and grateful to have something to keep her mind off of what was — or wasn't — going to be happening that night.

Their first stop was Gillespie's Garage. Charlie carried the bag of yams into the office and set it on the floor.

"How's it going?" he asked Pete.

"It'd be going a whole lot better if every pie I made didn't taste like dirty feet. I don't know what I'm doing wrong."

"Aunt Polly used maple syrup in her sweet potato pie and she put roasted pecans on top," Alice said.

"Maple syrup? No kidding! Thanks, I'm going to give that a try."

The next stop was the parsonage, where they found Reverend Flowers in his kitchen with a dish towel tied around his waist.

"Good gravy, what happened to you?" Charlie exclaimed when he saw the Reverend's red fingertips. "Did you cut yourself or something?"

"Cherries," said the Reverend, wiggling his stained fingers to demonstrate that they were all still working. "I had no idea how much work it was going to be to pit them."

"Aunt Polly taught me a little trick about pitting cherries," said Alice. "Use a paper clip. You just unfold it, stick it in, and pull the pit right out."

"How ingenious!" cried Reverend Flowers. "I can hardly wait to try it."

"Do you mind if I offer you another piece of advice?" Alice asked politely. "You might not remember this, but Aunt Polly won the Blueberry for her cherry pie last year. As far as I know, they've never given the prize to the same kind of pie two years in a row."

Reverend Flowers smiled and put his hand on Alice's shoulder.

"I've heard that there are some folks in town who've set their sights on winning the Blueberry this year, now that Polly's not here to do it, but I'm not one of them. Your aunt was a remarkable person and I miss her dearly. I got to thinking about her today and for some reason it made me want to make a cherry pie."

Alice felt better somehow knowing that the reason Reverend Flowers was baking a pie was because he missed Aunt Polly. That feeling grew even stronger after she and Charlie arrived at the Evanses' house.

"Well, will you look who the cat dragged in," said Mr. Evans when he opened the door. "Charlie I was expecting, but what a treat to see you, too, Alice."

"We brought you those bananas you asked for," said Charlie handing him the bunch.

"Shhhh!" said Mr. Evans, pressing a finger to his lips. "It's going to be a surprise. Delores is turning sixty tomorrow. Polly always made her a banana cream pie on her birthday, so I thought I'd give it a whirl this year. Sure wish I knew how your aunt made that meringue of hers."

"Add a little cream of tartar to the egg whites," Alice told him. "And raise the oven rack a notch to brown it."

"For someone who says she doesn't know how to bake a pie, you sure do know a lot about it," Charlie commented after they'd made their final delivery.

"I guess I must have soaked things up without realizing it," said Alice.

They had reached the corner where it was necessary for them to go their separate ways.

"Thanks for helping me today," said Charlie.

"You're welcome," Alice told him, but in her heart it was she who felt grateful. Not only for Charlie's friendship and the fact that he had fixed her bike chain and had been willing to pretend to ask Nora Needleman out on a date, but because that afternoon she had discovered her aunt Polly's spirit alive and well in all the kitchens in Ipswitch where pies were being baked for the right reasons.

"Good luck tonight," Charlie called back over his shoulder. "With J.Q."

Alice had been so busy delivering groceries and handing out free advice to people about baking pies that she'd actually succeeded in putting the plan out of her mind. But now the sun was beginning to set and one way or another it would all be over soon.

• • •

When Alice walked in the door there was an awful smell in the house and a hideous new pie sitting on the kitchen counter. Clearly *this* pie had not been made for the right reason.

"What kind is it supposed to be?" she asked her father, who was drinking a glass of tomato juice and circling ads in the Help Wanted section of the paper.

"I believe it's rhubarb," he said, shaking his head sadly. "Don't tell your mother I said this, but I don't recall Polly's rhubarb pie ever being quite that color, do you?"

"Where's Mom?" asked Alice.

"She's gone to bed with another headache. Doc Fyfe called in a prescription so she'll probably sleep right through 'til morning. I picked us up a couple of those newfangled TV dinners for tonight—Salisbury Steak or Chicken and Dumplings. Take your pick."

"Chicken, I guess," said Alice. "Is Lardo still here?"

"*Achoo!*" said her father by way of an answer. "I'll put those dinners in the oven as soon as I finish up here. Run along now and I'll call you when they're ready."

Alice and her father ate their TV dinners together in front of the television, but Alice was fidgety and kept asking what time it was until finally her father took off his watch and handed it to her.

"Some of us are trying to watch Bob Hope here," he said.

During the summer Alice's bedtime was nine o'clock, but by seven thirty that night she was tucked in bed with her teeth brushed and the light turned out. She lay awake for hours, nervously waiting. After a while when she heard her father come upstairs and get ready for bed she began to wonder if maybe it was time to give up. That's when she heard a rustling of leaves followed by the sound of her window being opened. A minute later the shiny black toe of a man's wing tip shoe appeared on the sill.

Alice's heart began to race. Had she been wrong about Miss DeSoto? Was it someone else who was after the recipe? A *man*?

"Pssst. Alice. Are you awake?"

Alice turned on the light and sat up in bed.

"Charlie Erdling, what are you doing here?"

"I thought you might need a backup," he said. "I've been sitting out in that tree for the past three hours. I wore dark colors so nobody would spot me."

"Where did you get those shoes?" Alice asked.

"I outgrew my old ones so Mom picked these up for me at the Salvation Army store. I don't know why somebody would give away a perfectly good pair of shoes."

"Probably because they pinched," said Alice. "Did you see anybody outside?"

"I know you don't want to hear this," Charlie said, "but I don't think J.Q. is coming."

Alice's heart sank.

She couldn't believe this was happening again. Was she never going to learn? None of her hunches had been right — why did she think it would be any different this time?

"Where's Lardo?" asked Charlie.

Alice had just pointed under the bed, when they heard a branch snap outside. Alice and Charlie looked at each other. Another snap sent Charlie skittering across the room into the closet to hide. Alice turned off the light and lay back down in her bed to wait.

A few minutes later, a shadowy figure slipped through the window, crossed quickly to the bed, and hesitated slightly before slowly sliding a hand under Alice's pillow. That's when Lardo made his surprise attack. Charging out from under the bed, fangs bared and back arched, he leapt at the intruder with a terrifying hiss. Alice turned on the light, and Charlie came busting out of the closet screaming bloody murder. In a flash the woman, dark haired and dressed head to toe in black, was out the window again, but Charlie grabbed her by the legs and hung on for dear life. Alice's parents came running when they heard the commotion.

"What's going on?" her mother cried. "Who's that hanging out the window?"

"It's the person who stole your pie, Mom. The same person who broke into the pie shop and catnapped Lardo and stole Aunt Polly's key and —"

"Can you hurry it up?" said Charlie. "I don't think I can hold on to her much longer."

"I knew you wouldn't believe me unless you saw it with your own two eyes, Mom," said Alice. "This time the jig really is up. Pull her in, Charlie."

Charlie pulled the woman kicking and screaming back into the room. When Alice's mother saw who it was, she gasped.

"Jane Quizenberry!" she exclaimed. "The Blueberry Bridesmaid!"

● ● ●

The police were called and Miss Quizenberry was taken down to the station for questioning. Chief Decker sent a couple of his men up to the Ipsy Inn with flashlights to recover the chocolate cream pie. They found a number of interesting things in Miss Quizenberry's suitcase, including the key to Polly Portman's pie shop, two wigs — one white, one blond — and a bottle of sleeping powder. Miss Quizenberry had sprinkled the powder on some cat food in order to make it possible for her to examine Lardo without being scratched. She was convinced for some reason that Polly had tattooed the piecrust recipe on his belly.

• • •

After the police left, Mr. Anderson drove Charlie home. Alice's mother came and sat beside her on the bed. She was holding a scrapbook filled with articles about Polly and her pie shop. Included were thirteen black-and-white photographs taken at the American Pie Makers Association award ceremonies after Polly had given her Blueberry acceptance speeches. Polly stood smiling in her leopard-print hat, holding up her gold medal for the camera. Next to her in each photograph Alice was surprised to see Jane Quizenberry, looking extremely disappointed.

"What's she doing there?" asked Alice when her mother showed her the photographs. "And what's that little round thing in her hand?"

"It's a silver Blueberry. That's what they give to the people who win Blueberry Honors," she said. "Jane Quizenberry was a runner-up so many times the press gave her a nickname. They called her 'The Blueberry Bridesmaid.'"

"What does that mean?" asked Alice.

"'Always a bridesmaid, never a bride' is an expression. I guess I'm not the only one who felt she was living her life in Polly's shadow."

"Where did you find this?" Alice asked, slowly turning the pages of the scrapbook. "Was it in the pie shop?"

"No," her mother answered simply. "It belongs to me. It's been here all along."

"Did Aunt Polly know you were saving all this stuff?"

"She probably would have thought it was silly. Polly didn't care about being famous. She didn't even really like it. All she wanted to do was make pies."

"If I tell you something, do you promise you won't get mad?" asked Alice. "I don't think you're going to win the Blueberry this year, Mom."

"Did you happen to see the rhubarb pie I made this afternoon?"

"Yes, but I don't think—"

"That you've ever seen a more beautiful pie in your entire life?"

Alice didn't know what to say—then she saw the corners of her mother's mouth begin to twitch and realized to her great relief that she had been kidding.

"I only wish you could have seen the look on your father's face when he saw it," she said with a giggle. "I thought he was going to cry."

"Does this mean you won't be baking any more pies?" asked Alice hopefully.

"Can you ever forgive me?" Alice's mother asked. "I've been such a fool. I wasted so much time envying Polly's gift, I somehow lost sight of the greatest gift I've ever been given — you."

Alice lay her head in her mother's lap.

"Will you stay with me, Mom?" she asked. "Until I go to sleep?"

"Of course I will," said her mother.

There was something else Alice wanted, something she'd been thinking about for a long, long time.

"Will you sing to me?" she whispered.

Alice closed her eyes and her mother began to sing. She really did have the voice of an angel. High and pure and as she sang, Alice's heart unclenched, and something warm flowed into the spaces inside her that had been aching and empty since Aunt Polly had passed. The next morning when Alice woke up, her mother was still there, and curled up next to them on the bed, was Lardo — purring.

PEACH PIE

6 ripe Red Haven peaches, peeled and slivered
½ cup brown sugar
¼ cup sugar
¼ cup instant tapioca
2 TBS crystallized ginger, finely chopped
½ tsp ground cinnamon
1 TBS butter

Mix ingredients together — reserving butter. Pour
into unbaked, pricked pie shell. Dot with butter.
Cover with lattice-top crust. Bake at 450 for 10
minutes, then reduce temperature to 350 and bake
until done — about 45 minutes.

*Reminder — as if I need one. Alice's favorite. (Birthday:
March 18)*

Chapter Twelve

A couple of days later, Charlie Erdling showed up at Alice's house with a paper bag full of peaches.

"They're Red Havens," he told Alice. "The same kind your auntie always used. I saw them at the A&P this morning and it came to me in a flash."

"What came to you in a flash?" asked Alice.

"We ought to make a pie."

"Oh, no," said Alice, covering her face. "You're not thinking about trying to win the Blueberry now, too, are you? Isn't it enough that we got our pictures on the front page of the paper?"

The Ipsy News had printed a big picture of Alice and Charlie standing arm in arm under the headline *REAL LIFE SKY KING AND PENNY SOLVE LOCAL MYSTERY.*

"I wasn't thinking about the Blueberry," said Charlie. "I was thinking about my grandma's perfume. Since peach was your favorite pie, I thought maybe if we made one, the smell of it would do the trick for you."

That was the moment when Alice knew for sure that she and Charlie Erdling would be friends for the rest of their lives.

"I have something to show you," Alice said.

She led Charlie out into the kitchen and handed him a battered old cigar box. Inside were dozens of folded-up pieces of paper, all of them stained and tattered from years of use.

"Aunt Polly's recipes," Alice told him. "The police found them in Jane Quizenberry's suitcase."

Charlie's eyes got very wide.

"Is the secret piecrust recipe in here?"

Alice shook her head.

"No," she said, lifting one of the papers from the box and unfolding it, "but this one is."

It was the recipe for Aunt Polly's peach pie. On the bottom, she'd written: *Alice's favorite.*

•   •   •

Polly had always started by making the crust, but since there wasn't a recipe for that in the cigar box, Alice found one in a cookbook.

"It says here use thirty-four cups of vegetable shortening," Charlie said, reading from the book.

Alice leaned over his shoulder and looked at the page.

"That says *three-quarters* of a cup," she told Charlie.

"Maybe it would be better if I just watched," he said.

Alice sent Charlie to the pantry for the can of LARDO! while she gathered the other ingredients for the crust. Following the directions, she mixed flour, shortening, salt, and water together until it formed a ball. It didn't look exactly the way Aunt Polly's pie dough had looked, but it was close enough. When she had finished, she sprinkled flour on the counter and, using the new rolling pin her mother had purchased, she began to flatten the dough into a round crust. Carefully lifting the edge with a spatula, she gently folded the circle over her forearm, to keep it from tearing as she transferred it into a pie plate; then she pricked the bottom five times and set it aside.

"Wow," said Charlie. "You're good."

Lardo wandered in at that point and started yowling to be fed.

"You want me to fry him up some sardines?" asked Charlie.

"He already ate," Alice said. "Mom falls for it every time. She's a total pushover just like Aunt Polly was."

As soon as Lardo realized Alice wasn't going to feed him, he quit the starvation act and waddled out of the kitchen, his big belly dragging along the linoleum. As he passed through the living room, Alice's father sneezed.

"Good morning, Lardo," he said from behind his newspaper.

Alice rolled out a second crust and with a table knife she carefully cut it into narrow strips.

"What's that for?" asked Charlie.

"We're going to make a lattice top later."

"*We?*" said Charlie.

"I'll show you how. It's easy."

Next it was time to prepare the peaches for the filling.

"Your auntie's recipe says they're supposed to be peeled, but it doesn't say how to do it."

It was almost as if Aunt Polly was there inside Alice's head, telling her what to do.

"Like this, Alice. Remember?"

Alice placed a peach in a big slotted spoon and lowered it into a bowl of hot water. She counted slowly to twenty, then she lifted the peach out and put it into the bowl of cold water Charlie had filled and placed on the counter for her. She counted to twenty again, then she removed the peach and held it in her hand.

"Good gravy," said Charlie as Alice slipped the loosened skin off with her fingers, revealing the glistening yellow flesh beneath it. "It's like magic."

"Your turn," said Alice, handing Charlie the spoon.

When they had removed all the skins, Alice's mother joined them in the kitchen just long enough to help cut up the peaches and chop the crystallized ginger. After that, Alice measured granulated sugar and sprinkled it over the sliced peaches. Then she showed Charlie how to scoop brown sugar out of the box and pack it down in a measuring cup with the back of a spoon. They used a set of little tin spoons to measure the cinnamon and tapioca pearls.

"Now what?" asked Charlie.

Alice poured the peaches into the pie pan and lay four strips of dough across the top. Then she handed Charlie a long strip and told him to start in the center.

"Weave it over one and under the next until you get to the other side."

Alice had to help, but eventually Charlie caught on.

"That was fun!" he said when they were finished.

Alice carefully slipped the pie into the oven. The lattice was uneven, and she'd had trouble getting the edges of the crust to hold together properly when she crimped them, but it didn't matter. She was proud of the pie she and Charlie Erdling had made, and she smiled, remembering something Aunt Polly had told her once —

"The most important ingredient in a pie is the love that goes into making it."

•   •   •

Alice had just set the oven timer when the doorbell rang.

"I'll get it!" she heard her mother call.

"Good afternoon, Mrs. Anderson," said a man with a deep voice. "Allow me to introduce myself. My name is Gerald P. Hammerschlacht. President of Hammerschlacht Products and Services out of Cincinnati, Ohio."

Hammerschlacht. Why did that name sound so familiar to Alice?

"Whatever it is you're selling, Mr. Hammerschlacht, I'm afraid we're not buying today," said Alice's mother. She started to shut the door.

"Who is it, Ruthie?" Alice's father called from the living room.

"Salesman," she called back.

"Wait," said the man. "I do apologize for not being more clear about the purpose of my visit. I assure you, I'm not here to sell you anything."

Then he told her that he was sorry that he'd missed the funeral; he'd been away in Europe on business. Now he had come to pay his condolences and to thank the entire Anderson family on behalf of LARDO! for Polly Portman's generous gift.

"What do you mean, on behalf of Lardo?" Alice's mother asked. "Do you know Lardo?"

The man chuckled. "*Know* it? Why, I invented it!" he said proudly. "LARDO! vegetable shortening is the cornerstone of Hammerschlacht Products and Services, and I expect our sales will be even higher now, thanks to your sister's generous gift."

"What gift?" asked Alice's father, who had joined his wife at the door now to see what was going on.

"The piecrust recipe," said Mr. Hammerschlacht. "I met with Miss Portman some years back, not long after she'd won the first of her Blueberry Awards. I'm here to honor my part of the agreement we made."

This was the point at which Alice's parents invited Mr. Hammerschlacht to come inside. A few minutes later, Alice's mother came into the kitchen, weeping uncontrollably, and asked Alice to come join them out in the living room.

"You're not going to believe it," she told Alice, hugging her tightly. "You're just not going to believe it."

RHUBARB PIE

8 cups cut rhubarb
1½ cups sugar
½ cup flour
2 TBS butter
cream
cinnamon sugar

Mix sugar and flour. Wash, string, and cut rhubarb
into ¾-inch pieces. Press unbaked piecrust into pie
pan and prick with fork. Place some of the sugar
mixture on bottom, then layer of rhubarb, repeat,
etc., until rhubarb mounds high; top with the
remaining sugar/flour mixture. Top with 2 table-
spoons of butter cut in small pieces. Place top
crust and seal edges and cut vents. Brush top crust
with cream. Sprinkle lightly with cinnamon sugar.

Bake at 425 for about 20 minutes, then reduce to 350
until bubbly and done. About 1 hour+ total cooking
time. Cool and serve with vanilla bean or honey ice
cream.

*Reminder: This is another one of those juicy pies that always
runs over, so make sure to place a jelly roll pan or a piece
of foil underneath it while it bakes.*

Chapter Thirteen

The reason Mr. Hammerschlacht's name had sounded familiar to Alice was because he was one of the two people Mr. Ogden had mentioned having witnessed her aunt Polly's will. Polly Portman had requested that Mr. Hammerschlacht be present when she signed her will, and then she had sent him back to Cincinnati with a copy of the piecrust recipe, which he promised to keep under lock and key until the day she died.

"I don't understand," said Alice. "I thought Aunt Polly left the recipe to Lardo."

"She did, honey," said Alice's mother. "Just not the way we thought she did."

It appeared that Mr. Odgen had missed a small but terribly important detail in Polly Portman's will. When he'd read the will aloud to Alice, he'd said that Polly had left her recipe to her beloved Lardo, and her beloved cat Lardo to Alice. But in fact what she'd written was that she'd left her recipe to her beloved LARDO! — and her beloved cat Lardo to Alice.

Polly Portman had a gift for pie making, and since her greatest pleasure was sharing that gift with others, she had decided that the best thing to do would be to leave her piecrust recipe to the company that made LARDO! so that they could print it on every single can. Anyone who wanted it could have the recipe now. But there was more. In exchange for the piecrust recipe, Mr. Hammerschlacht had agreed that after Polly passed, he would come to Ipswitch with two things in hand — a contract for Alice to write an advertising jingle for LARDO! and a contract for Alice's mother to sing it.

• • •

That afternoon after Mr. Hammerschlacht left, Alice went out to the kitchen and told Charlie everything that had happened.

"Good gravy!" he said. "Congratulations."

Alice felt a song coming on, but instead of pushing it away she sang it right out loud in front of Charlie.

A cat, a key, a clink, a clue,
A chocolate pie, a friend that's true,

A mystery that is finally through,
And now a happy ending, too.

Aunt Polly had sent her a message that day—one that she would never forget. Alice was a songwriter, and she was grateful for the gift she had. The fact that she was already on her way toward making her first million dollars was just a scoop of ice cream on the pie.

"If you want, I'll tell Nora Needleman I made you ask her to go to the movies with you," Alice offered later that afternoon. She and Charlie were playing a game of checkers on the living room floor.

"That's okay," said Charlie. "It's not like asking a girl to go to the movies means you have to marry her or anything."

Mrs. Anderson invited Charlie to stay for dinner. While Charlie called home to ask permission, Alice went out to the kitchen to check on the pie. When she opened the oven door, the smell of fresh-baked peach pie filled the room. It didn't smell the same as Aunt Polly's pie, and it certainly didn't look the same, but she knew in that instant that everything was going to be okay. She could almost feel Aunt Polly lean down and kiss her on the forehead.

"I'll miss you," Alice whispered.

And she was sure she heard Aunt Polly say—

"I'll miss you even more."

Dinner that night at the Andersons' house was meat loaf and mashed potatoes with gravy. For dessert there was peach pie. Alice's mother served up four slices.

"Looks delicious," said Alice's father, as he lifted his fork.

"It certainly does," said her mother.

Alice looked at her parents and smiled. She had wondered if she would ever feel happy again, and now she knew the answer.

Charlie touched the edge of his piece of pie, then licked his finger.

"Good gravy!"

"What's the matter?" asked Alice. "Is it awful?

"See for yourself," he said.

Alice took a bite of pie. The crust was a bit rubbery, and the filling wasn't nearly as good as Aunt Polly's had been, but to her surprise, it was actually not half bad.

"Pretty good," she said.

"What do you mean, pretty good?" Charlie cried. "It's great!"

And they all four burst out laughing.

• • •

In the fall of 1955, several important things happened. On Monday, September 5, a housewife in Haddonfield, New Jersey, won the Blueberry Award for her groundbreaking

Mississippi mud pie, thus ending Polly Portman's thirteen-year winning streak. Jane Quizenberry was not available for comment. In November, the town of Ipswitch got a new mayor. Henry Needleman decided he'd had enough of politics and didn't want to run for reelection. Since the VOTE FOR NEEDLEMAN posters were already printed up, Melanie simply pasted her picture over her husband's smiling face and won the election by a landslide. Right before Christmas, the new LARDO! jingle began playing on TV. Alice saw it for the first time on a Saturday morning during a commercial break on *Sky King*.

"Mom, Dad, come quick!" she shouted. "It's on!"

LARDO! you really oughta try it.
Buy it — betcha'll be a fan.
LARDO! makes a perfect pie dough.
If you wanna know the secret,
It's written on the can!
L-A-R-D-OH! OH! OH!
LARDO!

"Well, I'll be a monkey's uncle," said Alice's father, putting down his paper. "Ruthie, you sound like a dream. And, Alice, that tune of yours is downright catchy."

Alice's mother beamed and put her arm around her daughter.

"Did you notice, George? Every single one of those rhymes is perfect. Now, that's what I call *talent.*"

Alice and her mother had gone to New York City to record the jingle. While they were there, Alice sent Charlie a postcard of the Empire State Building. She signed it *Love, Alice.* When they returned home, Ruth Anderson went straight to Reverend Flowers to ask if maybe they could use another voice in the choir. She'd also started singing in the shower, which made everyone in the Anderson household very happy, especially Lardo, who sometimes liked to sing along.

Polly Portman had spent her whole life expressing gratitude for the gift she'd been given. She baked pies for the pure joy of it and delighted in the pleasure it brought to others. Alice could only hope that she would be able to live up to the example that had been set for her. Sitting on the couch that December morning, snuggled between her parents, Alice decided a good place to start might be right where her aunt Polly had left off.

"Thank you very much," she said, to no one in particular, and she meant it with all her heart.

Forty Years Later . . .

PEANUT BUTTER RASPBERRY CREAM PIE

½ cup peanut butter
½ cup powdered sugar
2 cups milk
1 egg yolk
3 TBS flour
¾ cup sugar
1 tsp vanilla
pinch of salt
1 small box raspberry Jell-O
2 cups raspberries (fresh or frozen)
whipped cream

Mix peanut butter and powdered sugar together till
it forms little balls. Put the mixture on the bottom
of a cooled prebaked crust.

Heat milk in saucepan. In separate saucepan, combine
egg yolk, flour, sugar, vanilla, and salt. Once milk
is heated, slowly add to flour and sugar mixture in
saucepan, stirring constantly. Continue stirring
until mixture comes to a boil. Cool, then pour on top
of peanut butter crumbs. Prepare a small box of red
raspberry Jell-O according to package directions.
Cool, then add about 2 cups raspberries to Jell-O
(can be fresh or frozen). Let Jell-O cool and thicken
slightly (it should be thick enough to be firm but
not so thick that it isn't pourable), then pour on
top of pudding. Add whipped cream and serve.

Epilogue

August 1995

Alice Anderson was standing on a step stool, rummaging around in the back of a high cupboard in the kitchen, doing a little spring cleaning even though it was the middle of August. The church was having a rummage sale, and Alice was hunting for her mother's old coffee percolator, which she thought she remembered having stashed up there. She didn't find the percolator, but what she did come across was Lardo's little blue china plate. In science fiction movies, time machines are always depicted as complicated metal contraptions with flashing lights and bundles of coiled wires coming out of the top, but that little blue plate transported Alice back in time to the summer of 1955 so fast it took her breath away.

The plate was dusty, and there was a dead fly lying on its back in the middle of it, so Alice climbed down and took it over to the sink to rinse it off. When she had finished drying the plate with a dish towel, she carried it outside to a big rock where she sometimes went when she needed a quiet place to think. It was a nondescript gray boulder in a shady corner of the backyard, near the rosebushes her mother had planted back when they had first built the new house. Alice's mother had passed away several years ago and her father had followed just six months later.

The house was much bigger than Alice needed it to be — it had four bathrooms, for heaven's sake! But thanks to the royalty money she got every time they played the LARDO! jingle on TV, the Anderson family had lived there together comfortably for years, and until the time came for Alice to join her parents and Aunt Polly in the great beyond, she couldn't imagine living anywhere else.

Sitting there on her rock, holding the little blue plate in her lap, the edges of Alice Anderson's world began to blur and grow soft as memories of her aunt Polly and the pie shop came flooding back. Alice could see her aunt standing in the doorway of PIE, waving, a crinkled fan of wrinkles unfolding at the corners of her eyes as she smiled and touched the brass key that hung around her neck. Alice had led a wonderful life, and she often wondered what her aunt would have thought about the way things had turned out.

Polly would have been happy that Alice and her mother had become so close, and she would have been glad that

Lardo had lived to the ripe old age of twenty-two. He was buried near the big gray rock where Alice was sitting. Although the Andersons had considered getting another cat after he passed, it didn't seem fair to put Alice's father through that again. He never got over his allergies, but even though Lardo made him sneeze, he'd cried right along with Alice and her mother when they'd finally had to put the old cat down. Alice was immersed in memories, lost in thought, when a sweet high voice pulled her back to reality.

"*Yoo-hoo!*"

"Over here, Polly!" Alice called.

Alice knew she wasn't supposed to have favorites, but secretly she did. Part of it was the name, of course, but the truth is little Polly was the kind of person people couldn't help but love, just like the remarkable woman she'd been named after.

"Dad says I finally got it right," Polly said. "But you're the expert. Taste."

Her bright red hair was pulled back in a high ponytail and she bounded across the yard to Alice, all legs and bony elbows, holding a pie plate in her hands. Polly was born on October 30, 1985, the same day Kirby Grant, the actor who had played Sky King, was killed in a car accident. At ten years old, she was the spitting image of her father, and Alice's heart swelled with love.

"Here." The girl pulled a fork out of her back pocket and handed it to Alice, then held out the pie. There were six tear-shaped vents on the top of the crust oozing golden juice, and the edges were crimped in even little waves. Alice knew what it was, and smiled.

"Start in the middle," the girl instructed.

Alice stuck the fork into the middle of the pie, scooped out a big bite, and put it in her mouth.

"What do you think?" asked the girl.

Alice's throat grew tight with emotion, and tears sprang to her eyes.

"Good gravy," said Polly. "Too much cinnamon, right?"

Alice shook her head as a single tear slid down her nose and fell into the pie.

"It's perfect," she said.

"Really?" asked Polly, flashing her father's wonderful grin. "No kidding? *Whoo hoo!*"

Polly was number three of five children, all of them redheads and mirror images of their father. Charlie Erdling and Alice had been best friends for forty years, but in the end, it was Nora Needleman who'd captured Charlie's big heart. Alice certainly hadn't seen it coming, but then life is like that sometimes. At first she was upset; she didn't think Nora deserved Charlie, but Charlie convinced her that she ought to give Nora a second chance, and eventually Alice and Nora became as close as sisters.

Like her aunt Polly, Alice never married. She had no children of her own, but the Erdling kids all called her Auntie Alice, and that was good enough for her. As it turned out, Nora surprised everyone by revealing a hidden talent for making pies. After they were married, Charlie and Nora bought the old pie shop and fixed it up again. They kept the name PIE, and on September 6, 1993, the welcome sign on the city limits of Ipswitch was repainted to read *14 Blueberries and counting!* Nora won the medal for her peanut butter raspberry cream pie. When she made her acceptance speech at the APA conference, she gave all the credit to her husband, Charlie, because he had been helping her in the kitchen when she'd made it, and had accidentally mixed up two recipes. With Polly Erdling coming up the pike, it looked like the pie business would be booming in Ipswitch for many years to come.

After Charlie's little Polly left that afternoon, Alice went upstairs to her bedroom, opened the closet, and took down the round red hatbox she kept on the top shelf. Wrapped in white tissue paper and smelling of mothballs was Aunt Polly's leopard-print hat. She carefully lifted it out of the box and put it on. Polly had loved that hat, and she had loved Alice, too, which was one of the luckiest things that had ever happened to either of them. Alice grabbed her purse and, still wearing the hat, strolled down to the A&P, where she bought a can of their finest sardines. When she got home, she fried up three of the salty fish, lay them side by side on the little blue china plate, and carried it out to the spot where Lardo was buried. Placing the plate in the grass, Alice sang a little song she'd been working on in her head.

How lucky am I to be right here,
How lucky am I indeed.
A lifetime of love and song and pie,
What more could a person need?

In the morning when Alice went out to check, the little blue plate was licked clean. When she told Charlie about it later, he laughed and said most likely it was a raccoon that had eaten the fish, but he had a hard time explaining away the ornery fat white cat that showed up on Alice's doorstep two days later, yowling indignantly to be fed.

PIE CREDITS

APPLE PIE ("Jim's favorite")
Recipe contributed by
Sarah Weeks of Nyack, New York

COCONUT CREAM PIE ("Eat off the floor")
Recipe contributed by
Page Laughlin of Winston-Salem, North Carolina

BUTTERMILK PIE
Recipe contributed by
Ann Sawtelle of San Antonio, Texas

GREEN TOMATO PIE
Recipe contributed by
Thomas B. Wilinsky of Callicoon Center, New York

SOUR CHERRY PIE
Recipe contributed by
Vikki Gremel of Seward, Nebraska

HUCKLEBERRY PIE
Recipe contributed by
Frances Weeks of Ann Arbor, Michigan

CHOCOLATE CREAM PIE ("Grandma Bell's")
Recipe contributed by
Grace Bell of Checotah, Oklahoma

LEMON CHESS PIE ("Aunt Jane's")
Recipe contributed by
Jane Q. Wirtz of Washington, DC

KEY LIME PIE
Recipe contributed by
Magaly Perez of Fremont Center, New York

CONCORD GRAPE PIE
Recipe contributed by
Kristie Miner of Maine, New York

PECAN PIE ("Tio's")
Recipe contributed by
Amy Roberts of Austin, Texas

PEACH PIE ("Damien's favorite")
Recipe contributed by
Jil Picariello of New York, New York

RHUBARB PIE
Recipe contributed by
June Fontaine of Eagle Bend, Minnesota

PEANUT BUTTER RASPBERRY CREAM PIE
Recipe contributed by
Ann Miller Yoder of Goshen, Indiana

THANK YOU VERY MUCH . . .

I'd like to express my deepest gratitude to David Levithan, Emily Van Beek, Holly McGhee, and my mother, Fran Weeks, for enthusiastically embracing *PIE* from the get-go. Jim Fyfe, thank you for your loving support and endless patience — I couldn't have written this book without you. Lastly, thank you to Parish Finn and Charlotte Steiner, who are wise beyond their years; to my son, Gabriel, who lent a crucial last-minute ear; and to the many generous friends and family members who were willing to share their favorite pie recipes with me.

Sarah Weeks made all fourteen pies that she included in this book, though the recipes came from all over the country. Ultimately, she decided her favorite pie was cherry, with buttermilk coming in a close second.

When not wielding her rolling pin, Sarah is at her desk, writing widely acclaimed novels, including *So B. It*; *Oggie Cooder*; *Oggie Cooder, Party Animal*; and *As Simple As It Seems*. She lives in New York and can be found on the Web at www.sarahweeks.com.